Sonrise Stable
Rejoice With Me

Vicki Watson

Illustrated by
Janet Griffin-Scott, Julie Watson-Ables

Or what woman, having ten silver coins, if she loses one coin, does not light a lamp, sweep the house, and search carefully until she finds it? And when she has found it, she calls her friends and neighbors together, saying, 'Rejoice with me, for I have found the piece which I lost!'

Luke 15:8,9

Sonrise Stable Characters *(Horses in Parentheses)*

Grandma *(Kezzie)*

Lisa and Robert Kristy and Eric Julie *(Elektra)* and Jonathan

Lauren Rosie *(Scamper)* Jared *(Scout)*

Carrie *(Bandit)* Jessie *(Patches)*
Jamie *(Pearl)*

(co-own Majestic)

Billy: Nineteen-year-old employee of Sonrise Stable *(Sassy)*

Sonrise Stable horses: Cadence, Charley, Nikki, Chester, Coolidge

Cats: June Bug, Katy, Jemimah, Cowboy, Sparrow

Dog: Tick

Chapter 1

Lost Money

Rosie leaned over the side of the bed and pressed one hand against the hardwood floor. With the other, she aimed a flashlight into the back, left corner.

"Is it under there?" Carrie asked.

Rosie slowly panned the light to the right. "No. Just lots of dust bunnies."

Carrie dropped to her hands and knees, her head nearly touching Rosie's. "Dust bunnies? More like dust ponies! Do you ever sweep in here?"

Rosie placed both hands on the floor, kicked her legs up and over and flipped off the bed to a standing position.

Carrie shook her head. "I wish I could do that."

"It's easy. I'll teach you some time." Rosie walked over and yanked her desk drawer open. "Keep looking. We have to find that money!"

Carrie opened the top drawer of the dresser and pawed through Rosie's socks. "Don't you remember where you put it?"

Rosie paused in the middle of emptying the desk. "Seriously? If I remembered where I put it, do you think we'd both be searching for it right now?"

Carrie threw a balled-up pair of socks at her sister.

Rosie ducked and slammed the desk drawer shut. She placed both hands on the top of her head and squeezed. "Think, think. If was a hundred dollar bill, where would I hide?"

"If I was a hundred dollar bill, I wouldn't be hanging out with a crazy person like you," Carrie laughed.

When their friend, Katrina, and her father had come to pick up her horse, Baron, Mr. Taylor had handed Rosie an envelope with two crisp new hundred dollar bills in it. One for her and one for Carrie—payment for the extra care they had provided for Katrina's horse.

The money was a surprise—the girls would have taken care of Baron for free. Summer camps were in full swing at that time, and they were all crazily busy, however, Rosie distinctly remembered running up to her room to put the money in a safe place. But now she couldn't remember where that safe place was. She felt even worse because she hadn't just lost her money; she had lost Carrie's too.

"I can't believe I lost it." Rosie plopped down in the middle of the floor and scanned around the room. "It has to be here somewhere."

"It's okay. Mr. Taylor didn't have to pay us anyway."

"No. It's not okay. I'm going to find it. We need that money if we're going to buy Mom and Dad an anniversary present."

Carrie sat down beside her sister. "Fifteen years is a long time to be married."

Rosie nodded, still looking for anything that would remind her of the hiding place. "And I need a new saddle pad for Scamper for the state trail ride."

Carrie rolled her eyes. "If we get in. We don't even know if our entries made it there in time."

"We'll get in," Rosie insisted. She had been training Scamper for the competition ever since the camps ended in mid August. Everyone had been so busy over the summer that the girls' mother thought Grandma had turned in the entries, and Grandma thought Kristy had sent them in. It turned out no one had.

There was a limit of one hundred riders in the competition—fifty juniors and fifty seniors. When Grandma realized what had happened, she called to see if the girls could still enter. There were still a few junior openings so Rosie and Carrie had immediately mailed in their forms and entry fees. Now they were waiting to hear whether the entries had been accepted.

"We have to get in," Rosie said. "Scamper needs to win his first real prize. Grandma said last year they gave away an endurance saddle for first place. I'd love to win that. Imagine how fast Scamper would be if he didn't have to carry his heavy western saddle!"

Rosie thought back to her first horse show. Scamper had performed so well, she was certain they would win—until Billy deliberately cut in front of them, causing her pony to break his gait. They ended up not even placing, while Billy won the class. Later that year Billy had apologized and given her the trophy and ribbon he had won, but it wasn't the same. Rosie wanted to really win something.

The bedroom door creaked open a little wider. Rosie looked over, expecting to see her mom or grandmother. Instead she saw June Bug, the bob-tailed calico, rubbing against the door. "How did you get inside, you little monster? You're supposed to stay outside now so you don't pick on Sparrow."

When Rosie scooted over to pet the cat, June Bug glared, ran past her and sprang up onto the desk.

Carrie continued searching through the dresser drawers. "She's so friendly."

"I don't even know why I try to be nice to that cat," Rosie sighed. "She hates me."

June Bug pawed at an ink pen and knocked it off the desk, peering over the edge to watch it clatter onto the floor. Rosie shook her head. "Why do cats love to do that?"

"Gravity experiments." Carrie nodded wisely.

"Yeah." Rosie laughed. "Somehow I don't think she's that brilliant."

The calico continued to prowl around on Rosie's desk. She batted at a small brown teddy bear with a red heart sewn on its tummy. June Bug glanced from one side to the other, then snatched the stuffed bear by the leg and jumped off the desk.

"Hey. Give that back!" Rosie leaped up and ran after her, but the cat scooted out the door. Rosie watched her escape down the stairs. "Did you see that? She took the bear Mom gave me!"

Carrie stared at the door for a moment. "You don't think…"

"Think what?"

"What if June Bug took the money?"

Rosie's eyes widened. "Oh no!" She held out both arms and let herself fall backward onto her bed. She lay there staring at the ceiling.

"If June Bug took it, it could be anywhere," Carrie moaned.

Rosie sat up and propped a pillow behind her. "When I was little, I used to blame things on June Bug."

"Everyone around here blames things on June Bug," Carrie laughed.

"Yes, but I'm the one who got it started."

"Really?" Carrie closed the last dresser drawer and brushed her hands off. "No money in there."

"It all started when I broke a vase at Grandma's. I was about five. I accidentally knocked it off the table, and it kind of split in two."

"Kind of? How can you 'kind of' break a vase?"

Rosie ignored her sister's question. "I panicked and hid the pieces behind a chair in the living room."

"Yeah, like that would fix everything." Carrie jumped onto the other end of the bed and sat facing her sister.

"Hey, come on. I was only five," Rosie said. "But, of course, Grandma found it and asked me what happened."

"And you confessed?"

"W-e-l-l," Rosie stretched the word out. "Not ex-act-ly. June Bug happened to be curled up in the recliner. As I stared at her, this wonderful idea began to form in my mind."

"Your little five-year-old mind?"

"Yes. It seemed quite believable to me at the time. I pointed to June Bug and told Grandma that the cat did it."

Carrie shook her head. "June Bug broke the vase? And put it behind the chair?"

"Yep." Rosie nodded. "My plan didn't work out too well though. Grandma looked at me sadly. Then when Mom and Dad came to pick me up, I had to tell the story again. With Grandma, it had just popped out of my mouth, but when I had time to think about it, it was a lot harder to deliberately lie to my parents. Before we got home, I started crying and had to tell them the truth."

"I figured you would." Carrie smiled. "I wish we had known each other when we were five."

"Me too. Then I could have blamed you!" Rosie tossed the pillow at Carrie and bounced herself off the bed. "It became a family joke after that to blame everything on June Bug."

Instead of firing the pillow back at her sister, Carrie rested her head on it. "Hmm, I never realized June Bug was such a criminal. Maybe she really did steal our money."

"Nah, I doubt it. Remember during the summer camps? We hardly ever saw her. I think she spent the whole summer in the hayloft hiding from all the kids."

Carrie smiled. "Especially Annabelle."

"Definitely. I wonder how she's doing?" Rosie missed the campers and all the activity of the summer.

"You're probably right." Carrie said. "Hey, I know you want to find the money, but can we take a break for a few minutes so you can read my latest story?"

Rosie took one last look around the room. "I suppose."

Carrie ran across the hall and returned with a spiral-bound notebook. "You can think about what kind of illustrations you want to do for it. I mean—if you think it's good enough. It's funny that June Bug came in here today. She's a big part of the story."

"You could write a whole book about that cat." Rosie took the tablet Carrie held out to her. "She is fun to draw, with that stubby poof-ball of a tail."

Rosie sat down, opened the tablet and began reading silently. She turned the first page and raised her eyes to see Carrie staring at her. "What are you doing?"

"Watching you read."

"I figured that. But why?"

"So I can tell if you like the story or not."

"I'll tell you if I like it."

"You don't have to tell me. I'll know by the way you look when you read it."

Rosie slapped the notebook shut. "Carrie, I can't concentrate with you staring at me like that! Why don't you look for my sketchpad? Maybe I already have some drawings we can use."

Carrie slowly stood up and walked away. Rosie resumed reading. Every once in a while she chuckled, and a few times she laughed out loud. Finally she closed the tablet to find Carrie once again seated at the foot of the bed staring at her.

"This is good!"

"You really think so? You're not just saying that because you're my sister?" Carrie took the tablet from Rosie.

"No. It is good. I think it's the best one you've written so far."

Carrie beamed as she thumbed through the pages. "I thought this would make a good illustration here, where Charley is eating the popcorn."

Rosie nodded. "That would be fun to draw."

Carrie handed the sketch pad to her.

"I haven't had a chance to draw since…" When Rosie flipped the cover open, something fell to the floor.

"Ha! You're kidding!" She bent down and picked up a long narrow envelope with the words, "Keystone Bank" printed in large letters down the side. She tore into the envelope. There were the two crisp, green bills.

"I remember now!" She handed one to Carrie. "I put them in here because I usually draw every day. I figured I wouldn't lose them that way."

"Come on!" Carrie jumped off the bed. "We have to tell everyone we found the money."

Rosie grabbed the bill from her sister. "Let's keep them in here." She opened the wide, middle desk drawer, placed the money inside, and slid it shut. "Now that we both know where it is, we won't lose it again."

"Does June Bug know how to open drawers?"

Rosie looked at the door where the cat had disappeared. "Hmm, with that cat you never know." She opened the drawer and took the money back out. "Let's get Grandma to keep it for us."

Rosie led the way out the door and down the stairs. "Now we have to decide what to get Mom and Dad for their anniversary."

Chapter 2

Lost Sheep

Jared walked back and forth across the large meeting room in the activity building as he read aloud from his Bible. "What man of you, having a hundred sheep, if he loses one of them, does not leave the ninety-nine in the wilderness, and go after the one which is lost until he finds it?"

He nodded to Carrie, and she read the next verse.

"And when he has found it, he lays it on his shoulders, rejoicing."

Rosie continued. "And when he comes home, he calls together his friends and neighbors, saying to them, 'Rejoice with me, for I have found my sheep which was lost!'"

Jared stopped in front of Billy and looked at him expectantly. "Do you get it?"

"Get what? The guy lost his sheep, found it, and then threw a big party."

Jared rolled his eyes and sat down beside Billy at the table.

Carrie was still surprised at the dramatic change in Jared since he'd been saved at the end of their first summer camp. Earlier that summer, he had been mad at Rosie because she kept pestering Billy about becoming a Christian. Now it seemed all Jared ever talked about was his faith. Grandma said he was going to make a fine preacher some day.

A few days after the last camp they started a Bible study that met once a week in the activity building. The big room seemed rather empty with just the four of them. Usually their cousin, Lauren, and Jared's twin sisters, Jessie and Jamie, joined them. Lauren and her mother, Lisa, were on their way to Texas to pack up the house they had sold recently, and the twins were sick. Rosie and Jared planned to invite other kids eventually, but for now they were focusing their efforts on Billy.

"Would you read verse 7?" Jared pointed out the location in Billy's Bible.

Carrie noticed that it was the study Bible Grandma had passed out to the kids during camp. The Bible looked pretty worn already. Was Billy actually reading it? Maybe he had slept on it or something.

"I say to you..." Billy read hesitatingly.

Carrie kept her eyes glued to her own Bible. She didn't want Billy to think she was staring at him. It must be awful to not be able to read well. She loved to read and wanted to write her own books some day. Billy had told them he couldn't ever remember reading a book—not even in school. He was able to pass tests just by listening in class.

"...more joy in heaven over one... sinner..." Billy stopped. "Hey, are you calling me a sinner?"

"I'm not." Jared shook his head. "But God is. He wrote the book. We're all sinners." He looked at the girls for confirmation, and they both nodded.

Billy closed his Bible and set it on the table. "I'm not a bad person." He crossed one of his long legs over the other and flicked the rowel of his spur with a finger to start it spinning. "I mean, it's not like I've killed anyone or anything like that."

"Hey, listen to this!" Rosie highlighted a few lines in her Bible with a colored pencil, then began reading aloud. "Or what woman, having ten silver coins, if she loses one coin, does not light a lamp, sweep the house, and search carefully until she finds it? And when she has found it, she calls her friends and neighbors together, saying, 'Rejoice with me, for I have found the piece which I lost!'"

She looked up. "Does that remind you of anything?"

Carrie smiled. "That sounds exactly like you yesterday when you couldn't find our money—I mean all except the sweeping part."

"Very funny." Rosie made a face at her sister. "Remember how excited we were to tell Mom, Dad and Grandma about finding the money?"

"It's going to be even more exciting when we tell them that this lost sheep—" Jared pointed to Billy—"has been found."

Billy slapped both hands on his legs, leaned forward, and pushed his tall, thin frame up out of the chair. He started toward the door. "I'm sorry, guys. I really don't have time for this. This stuff doesn't make sense to me. Anyway I have to get things ready for the new boarder arriving this afternoon."

Jared hurried after him. "Wait! Can we pray together before you leave?"

"Nah." Billy shook his head. "Maybe some other time." He walked out the door.

Carrie felt awful when Jared turned around and she saw the sad look on his face. He and Rosie had tried so hard to help Billy understand.

"Why doesn't he get it?" Jared pushed his baseball cap back and ran his fingers through his short hair. "I guess I'm not explaining it clearly enough."

"Maybe he needs to hear it from someone besides us," Rosie suggested.

Carrie smiled. "Wasn't there a donkey in the Bible that talked to some guy?"

"Oh yeah! I remember that," Rosie said. "Wouldn't it be great if God made Sassy talk to Billy? Then he would have to believe!"

"Hmm." Jared rubbed his chin and thought for a moment. "If Billy won't come to the Bible study, the Bible study will have to come to Billy—by way of Sassy."

Carrie watched a smile spread across her cousin's face. What was he thinking? She had a bad feeling it was going to be something that could get them all in trouble.

Jared looked around as if there might be someone lurking in the shadows, spying on them. He wiggled his finger. "Come here. I have an idea."

The girls gathered on each side of him, and in a hushed voice he explained his plan.

Carrie sat on a tack box watching Rosie sweep the barn aisle. The new boarder was supposed to have arrived at four. It was now a quarter till five. They had learned from Grandma that the boarder was a girl from one of the other

12

4-H clubs in the county. Carrie and Rosie both hoped it was someone they could be friends with. They missed Katrina since she and Baron had moved to Florida. Another former boarder, Hannah, was married now and had taken her blind horse, Dusty, to her new home. With the summer camps over, it was pretty quiet around the stable.

There wouldn't be many boarders after this either. The camps had been so successful that the family planned to focus their efforts on those and only take in a limited number of boarders. That would give them room to add more camp horses.

Tick, the Rottweiler, ran into the barn and rested her head on Carrie's lap. "You miss all the attention from the campers, don't you?" She hopped up. "Come on. Let's play tug-of-war."

The girls had tried to teach Tick to fetch. She had little to no interest in that game, but tug-of-war was a different story. The dog couldn't get enough of it. They used a short, braided rope with a large knot tied in one end. Tick preferred the knotted end, which made it hard for the girls to hang on—especially when the dog jerked her head up and down and from side to side, play-growling the entire time.

"I think I hear a trailer!" Rosie started out the door.

Carrie dropped her end of the rope and followed Rosie. Tick shook her head a few more times, making the rope flop around. The dog was disappointed that Carrie wasn't playing anymore, but then she noticed the horse trailer coming down the drive. She dropped her end of the rope and ran out of the barn barking.

An SUV pulling a silver two-horse, bumper-pull trailer rolled past them and came to a stop. Close behind was a black truck pulling the largest camper Carrie had ever seen.

Billy joined the girls in front of the barn. "Diesel."

Carrie looked at him. "What?"

"The truck's a diesel. Listen to it purr. Diesel engines have a different sound. Would I love to have one of those!"

"Sounds more like a growl, than a purr," Carrie said. "Besides I'm more interested in the camper. Look at that thing!"

"Dapple gray," Rosie said.

Carrie laughed. It figured. Her sister didn't notice anything but the horse. You could just barely see its hindquarters and the top of a tail above the high back doors of the trailer, but it did appear to be dapple gray in color.

Billy walked over to greet the man who got out of the SUV. He stretched out his hand. "William King."

Carrie smiled. She'd never get used to hearing Billy called William. It sounded way too formal.

"I'm Jim," the man said. "Jim Miller." He turned around and looked at the horse trailer.

A tall, thin girl walked around the corner. She was deeply tanned and had dark hair.

"This is my daughter, Abigail."

Abigail smiled, but didn't speak.

"We have a stall ready for you." Rosie nodded toward the barn.

Abigail frowned and shook her head. "Do you have a corral? We just got back from a competition, and I don't

14

want him cooped up in a stall. He'll get all stiff." She opened the side door of the trailer and clipped a lead rope onto her horse's halter.

"Sure," Carrie said. "We'll show you where you can turn him out. What's his name?"

"Raja." The girl nodded to her dad, who unlatched the back door. The horse stepped backward out of the trailer and whinnied a greeting to the horses in the barn.

The woman who had driven the truck walked over and joined them. "You're looking as beautiful as ever, boy."

"Oh, Mom, you say that about every horse I have!"

Every horse? Carrie wondered how many horses Abigail owned. She couldn't imagine ever having a horse other than Zach. Carrie stared at Raja. He was one of the most beautiful horses she had ever seen. His coat was covered in dark dapples; his mane and tail were a dark gray. He was lean and fit, but not too thin. From the look of his dished face and arched tail, she was pretty certain he was an Arabian. She'd ask Rosie later. She didn't want to sound stupid in front of this new girl.

Rosie reached out to pet Raja. "What kind of competition were you in?"

"I won a ten-mile race today." Abigail backed Raja away from the girls. "I'm a competitive trail rider."

"Oh, really?" Rosie said. "My sister and I are competing in the state 4-H trail ride next month."

"Guess I'll see you there. Or," she turned and looked at her dad, "you'll see Raja's tail, I mean." The two laughed together.

Rosie stared at her. "You're in the 4-H ride?"

"Raja and I won the junior division last year." Abigail swatted a fly away from her horse's neck. "My goal is to win it again this year. Next year I'll compete for the first time as a senior. I plan to win that too, but I might need a new horse to do it."

"Oh, honey, I thought you wanted to keep this one." Mrs. Miller rubbed Raja's forehead. "He's such a sweetheart, and you've been winning a lot of races with him."

"Now, Margaret—" Mr. Miller closed and latched the trailer door. "If the girl needs a new horse, she'll have a new horse. It's not like we don't have the money."

Abigail turned away from her mom and smiled at her father.

New horse? Carrie didn't understand this. She loved her horse, Zach. What did Abigail do? Get a new horse for every competition? Raja was so beautiful. How could she even think about parting with him?

Rosie motioned toward the new boarder. "Come on, Abbie, I'll show you where the corral is."

The girl stiffened and didn't move. "Um. It's Abigail. No one calls me 'Abbie'—not even my parents. I despise the sound of that name."

Oh, no. Carrie looked over at her sister, half expecting an angry outburst, but Rosie turned away and started toward the corral. Carrie hurried to catch up with her and leaned in close so she could whisper, "Why'd you say we were in the trail ride? We still don't know whether we got in or not."

Rosie kept her eyes focused straight ahead. "We'll get in, and Scamper and I will beat those two. You wait and see."

Chapter 3

Jared's Plan

Rosie stepped out of the stall and hung the pitchfork from a hook on the wall. She stretched and yawned. She wasn't naturally a morning person, however the horses were used to being fed early. As soon as Carrie finished, they would have their chores done and could get their horses out. The new girl had arrived early and was already tacking up her horse for a ride.

Raja was in the cross ties in the middle of the barn aisle. Rosie studied the horse. He was stunningly beautiful. He seemed bored and kept trying to get the end of one of the tie ropes into his mouth.

"What are you doing, boy? Are you hungry?" Abigail stepped past the horse's head to speak to Rosie. "Did you give him two scoops of grain this morning?"

Rosie pretended not to hear her. She spotted a baling twine on the floor and bent down to pick it up. The girl seemed to think she was a servant. Rosie tried to remain patient. She knew this was all part of working at Sonrise Stable.

Abigail grabbed her bridle from a hook on the stall door. She unfastened the buckle on the throatlatch. "I asked you if you fed him this morning. He's in training and needs to be fed properly in order to stay in top shape."

Rosie didn't like being interrogated, but her parents and grandmother insisted that she and Carrie treat the boarders politely. "Yes, of course we fed him. My sister and I feed the horses almost every morning."

The thought briefly crossed her mind that she could skip Raja's grain or feed him less. That might give her a better chance at winning the trail ride. She rejected the idea immediately. It wouldn't be right. It wasn't Raja's fault his owner was obnoxious. Besides, she wanted to beat Abigail fair and square. That is, if they got in the race at all.

Rosie had asked her grandmother again about calling to see if their entries had arrived in time. Grandma promised the girls that if they didn't hear by the end of the week, she would call the 4-H office.

"The only reason we moved Raja here was because of your trails." Abigail slipped a snaffle bit into her horse's mouth. "We actually have a nicer stable at home."

Rosie rolled her eyes and bit her tongue. Did Abigail realize how snobby she sounded? When Katrina had first arrived at Sonrise Stable, Rosie had really disliked her too. It had taken a while, but eventually they became good friends. She couldn't imagine that ever happening with this girl.

Abigail unfastened the cross ties. "We don't have enough land to allow me to condition him properly."

Rosie nodded. "We have great trails. That's how Carrie and I keep Scamper and Zach in such good shape."

Abigail laughed. "Those fat little ponies? There's no breed better than Arabians at endurance racing. This guy can run all day and barely break a sweat."

It was difficult, but Rosie resisted the impulse to respond to the "fat" comment. She stared at the tall, sleek Arabian. He had a faraway look in his eyes as if he were dreaming about racing across the desert—maybe running away from Abigail. Did she and Scamper really have a chance to beat them? After all, Scamper's mother, Jet, was just a little mixed-breed pony.

She eyed the lightweight endurance saddle Abigail used on Raja. Rosie wanted one like that for Scamper. She had been saving for a new saddle, but now she needed to use some of that money for her parents' anniversary gift.

Carrie finished her stall and joined them in the aisle. "He's so beautiful. How long have you had him?"

"This is my second year with him. I'll probably get a new horse when I move up to the senior division next year."

"Why?" Rosie couldn't understand this girl. Didn't she care about her horse? She had raised Scamper from a foal and wouldn't part with him even if they came in dead last in the trail ride. She was pretty sure that wouldn't happen though. Scamper was a little on the chubby side, but he was surprisingly fast. Grandma said his extra weight was like a reserve fuel tank he could engage whenever he needed it.

"Why what?" Abigail flipped the reins up over Raja's neck.

"Why would you get rid of Raja? He seems like a great horse," Rosie said.

Abigail looked at Rosie blankly. "Yes. He is a great horse, but it's not like he's a pet or anything. There will be more competition at the next level, and I want to have the best chance of winning. My dad already found the horse he wants to buy for me." Abigail stepped closer to the girls and spoke in a loud whisper. "I'm not supposed to tell anyone, but my dad's going to pay thirty thousand dollars for the new horse."

Rosie's eyes nearly popped out of her head. She looked away, hoping Abigail hadn't noticed. She didn't want the girl to think she was impressed. Her grandmother had paid three hundred for Jet. And of course, they hadn't paid anything at all for Scamper. She couldn't imagine what kind of horse could be worth that much money. "If someone offered me thirty thousand dollars for Scamper, I wouldn't take it."

"Yeah, right." Abigail started toward the front door, with Raja following at her side.

"I mean it." Rosie insisted. "I wouldn't."

"Nobody in their right mind would offer you thirty thousand dollars for that fat pony," Abigail said without turning around. "So you don't have anything to worry about."

Stunned, Rosie watched her leave. Then she took a few steps down the aisle and yelled after her. "I wouldn't even sell him for a hundred thousand."

"Why do you let her get to you?" Carrie said.

"What do you mean?" Rosie whirled back around. "She doesn't *get* to me."

"Oh yeah?" Carrie pointed to Rosie's hands. She had twisted the baling twine repeatedly until it was in a tight knot.

Rosie looked down. She let go of one end, and the string began slowly unraveling. "Well, maybe she does a little." She tossed the twine into the trash barrel. "Come on; let's see if Jared's ready."

"Shh! Here he comes." Jared motioned toward the girls, and they all hurried down the aisle into their horses' stalls.

Billy swung the riding arena gate open. Rosie could hear his spurs jangling as he headed their direction. "You all ready to ride?"

Rosie peeked out Scamper's stall door. "Yep. We've been waiting on you."

"Somebody has to do some work around here so you guys can play around with your horses all day. Your dad and I finished fixing that broken fence in the west pasture this morning." He stopped outside Scamper's stall, put his hands on the bars and looked in. "We need to get busy if you and Carrie are going to have any chance of beating you-know-who in that race."

After Rosie finished picking out Scamper's hooves, she was surprised to see Billy still standing there. She couldn't wait to see if Jared's idea would work. "Let's try ten miles today. I think they're ready for it. Scamper always does better when Sassy is with us. He can't stand to have that mule in front of him."

"So you admit my mule is good for something?"

And for something else too, Rosie thought. She shook her head at Billy. Was he going to stand there talking all day?

"You think Sassy can go ten miles?" Jared was busy saddling his gelding, Scout. "If it's too much for her, you could ride my mom's horse today."

"Ha! You'll be eating my mule's trail dust all day." Billy moved down to Zach's stall. "Bandit, old buddy, how are you doing?"

What was this a family reunion or something? Rosie had never seen Billy so chatty. Zach had been Billy's pony before her dad bought him for Carrie. He was called Bandit then. Since Billy worked at Sonrise Stable now, he saw the horse every day. Why was he acting like he had just noticed him?

"Here's the plan," Billy stood outside Zach's stall. "Carrie, you have Zach sneak up, like a bandit, on him." He pointed to Rosie's pony. "That guy will 'Scamper' off as fast as he can, but he'll never be able to stay ahead of you."

"Was that supposed to be funny?" Rosie tossed the hoof pick into the tack bucket. "Don't be ridiculous. Go get your mule ready or we'll leave without you!"

"All right. All right. What's the big rush?" Billy sauntered down the aisle and unlatched Sassy's stall. "I've never seen—"

The moment the door slid open, a loud, obnoxious braying sound filled the air, followed by someone—or something—talking in the strangest-sounding voice Rosie had ever heard.

"What have I done to you?" the voice began. It sounded like a donkey might sound if it could speak, with extremely loud brays punctuating each sentence.

Sassy whirled around to face Billy, her eyes wide and ears straight up. Billy had a similar expression on his face.

"Why have you struck me these three times?" the voice asked.

"What in the world?"

Rosie stepped out of Scamper's stall so she could see Billy's reaction. Jared and Carrie joined her in the aisle. The shocked expression on Billy's face had all three of them laughing.

The donkey voice continued, "Repent, for the kingdom of heaven is at hand! Hee-haw!"

Billy pointed his finger at Jared and started toward him. "I should have known you wouldn't give up that easily."

Jared ducked away from him.

"Hee-haw. Unless you are born again, you cannot see the kingdom of heaven. Hee-haw!"

Rosie put her hands over her ears to block out the horrendous noise.

"All right, where is it?" Billy looked around the stall. "Turn that crazy thing off!"

Jared laughed. He pushed past Billy through the door and pressed a button on a device that was attached to the wall in the corner of the stall.

Billy petted Sassy to calm her. "And what exactly was that supposed to prove?"

"God spoke through a donkey once," Carrie explained. "We thought He might be able to use a mule this time." She pointed to Jared. "It was his idea."

"I figured that," Billy said. "A talking donkey? Really?"

Rosie nodded. "Numbers, chapter 22."

"Unbelievable." Billy shook his head. "How'd you do that anyway?"

Jared showed Billy the motion detector attached to the edge of the stall door. "As soon as you slid this open, it activated the magnetic reed switch wired to my Arduino that I connected to an old cassette player."

Billy removed the tape player from the wall. "Where'd you find the crazy voice?"

"That was me," Jared laughed. "I had to record it a dozen times to get it just right. It took me a long time to be able to do it without laughing. I had to do it when no one else was home so they wouldn't think I was crazy. Then I added some distortion with audio software."

Rosie was impressed. If Jared didn't become a preacher, he could work with computers. He was always inventing some contraption or writing a program to do something.

Billy turned the cassette player back and forth. "There's really a talking donkey in the Bible?"

All three nodded.

"I'll have to look that up."

Rosie smiled and returned to Scamper's stall. She was glad Jared hadn't given up on Billy. It didn't seem that the mule trick had worked, but at least Billy was thinking about God again. She wished she could think of some creative way to try to reach him.

When everyone had their horses—and mule—saddled, Rosie led the group out of the barn. Grandma was walking down the driveway toward them. Rosie waved to her.

Grandma waved back and continued sorting through a stack of mail. "Oh! Oh!" She held out an envelope and waved it back and forth. "Wait! It's here!"

Rosie's heart thumped. "You mean the trail ride?"

Grandma nodded and hurried toward them. She ran her finger under the flap and tore it open.

Rosie watched her pull out a piece of paper and begin to read silently. "Grandma, come on! Are we in?" She dropped Scamper's reins to the ground and ran over beside her, trying to see what the paper said.

Grandma fished around in the envelope and pulled out two armbands with the numbers 99 and 100.

"We're in?" Rosie shouted.

Grandma smiled and nodded. "Looks like you got the last two places!"

"Yes!" Rosie raised both arms and jumped up in the air. "We're in!" She mounted Scamper and glanced at her sister. What was wrong with Carrie? She wasn't even smiling.

Chapter 4

Conditioning

"Can we rest a while? Zach is tired."

Rosie glanced at her sister's palomino gelding. He was a little on the lazy side and had been known to fake lameness in order to get out of work. "He looks fine to me."

Billy stopped Sassy and turned to face the others. "You still have four weeks to finish getting them ready, Rosie. You don't have to do it all in one day."

Jared pointed up ahead. "Let's ride to the top of that hill and take a break."

Rosie frowned, but nodded. She had wanted to win the race before, but now it was even more important—she just had to beat Abigail.

Sassy broke into her high-speed bouncy mule trot, and Scamper immediately took off after her. Rosie was already in a bad mood, and this didn't improve it. She scolded her pony. He wasn't supposed to move until she told him to. After weeks of hauling campers around the trails that summer, he had learned to pay more attention to the horse in front of him than to his rider. She would have to work on that.

The horses picked up a canter going up the slope. Rosie smiled in spite of herself. She loved Scamper's canter. It was so rhythmic and comfortable, even smoother than the rocking horse she had ridden for miles when she was a little girl. When they reached the top of the hill, a slight breeze rustled through the leaves. Rosie knew wearing a riding helmet was important, but she'd never had one that didn't make her head and face start sweating almost instantly. The cool breeze passing over her damp face was like stepping into instant air conditioning.

Rosie kicked her feet out of the stirrups, jumped down and faced Scamper. She reached under his head, running her fingers along the inside of his jaw. *No.* She shook her head and slid her fingers along the bone. *Nope.* She felt again. *Ah, there it is.*

She was getting faster at finding the point where the artery crossed over his jawbone. Scamper's pulse was pounding. She looked at her watch and counted each beat. "One, two, three…" Count for thirty seconds, then multiply by two. "Ninety. Not too bad."

Next she stared at Scamper's flank. His side expanded every time he took a breath. She counted again. When another thirty seconds had passed, she multiplied by two.

"Eighty-six? What?" She frowned. That was too high. She had expected it to be about sixty after a ride like this. She looked him over trying to determine what would cause his respirations to be that high. When she walked over to Scamper's right side, she noticed Carrie leaning against a tree. "Did you take Zach's pulse?"

"No. I couldn't find it."

"So you gave up? You know you have to keep a conditioning record for the trail ride with all your pulse and respiration figures recorded." Rosie had shown Carrie several times where to find the pulse—along his jaw as she had just done with Scamper or on the inside of his leg near the knee. She led Scamper over and helped Carrie locate the spot again. She couldn't understand why her sister wasn't more excited about the competition. Rosie couldn't wait for it. In fact she hadn't been able to think about much of anything else for the past few weeks.

"What are Scamper's vitals?" Billy asked.

Rosie reached out and petted Sassy's nose. "Ninety and eighty-six."

"Not good." Billy shook his head. "I think you're pushing him too hard too soon. You don't want him to invert—especially during the competition."

Jared led Scout over toward them. "I've ridden that trail before with my mom. It's rocky and has a lot steeper hills than here."

Carrie finished taking Zach's pulse. "What is inversion again?"

This was something else Rosie had gone over several times, but she patiently explained once more. "Normally a horse's heart rate is four times as fast as his breathing. Scamper's pulse when he's not exercising is usually forty beats per minute, but he only breathes ten times a minute."

Carrie nodded.

"If his breathing rate becomes higher than his pulse rate, that's being inverted."

"Oh, yeah, now I remember. I just have a hard time remembering which one is supposed to be higher."

"It's easy." Rosie squashed a fly that landed on Zach's neck and wiped her hand off on her jeans. "Think about yourself. Your heart beats seventy times per minute. If you breathed that often, it would be more than one breath every second." Rosie took several breaths in rapid succession. "Is that how you usually breath?"

Carrie laughed. "No. You're going to hyperventilate if you keep that up."

"Exactly." Rosie resumed breathing normally. "That's why you don't want your horse to invert."

"Okay. I get it now." Carrie felt under Zach's jaw again. "Now I need to get better at finding the spot where I can feel his pulse."

"If Scamper inverts during the competition, you'll lose points—and you'll have to stay at the checkpoint until he's not inverted, so you lose time as well," Billy said.

"I know." Rosie frowned. If Scamper nearly inverted on these trails, what would he do on the more challenging trails at the competition? She would have to step up his training to get him in better shape. Maybe she should start feeding him more grain. Would that give him more energy—or just make him chubbier?

"It's too bad you and Sassy can't be in the race," Rosie said. "With Sassy in front of him, Scamper wouldn't care how steep the hills were; he'd do anything to get in front of you."

"We are going to be in it."

"What?" Rosie stared at him. Billy was too old to be in 4-H now. What was he talking about? He couldn't be in the ride.

Billy smiled and patted Sassy. "I signed up to be a lag rider."

"Ah." Rosie nodded. Lag riders rode behind the competitors as a sort of safety net in case anything happened to a horse or rider. "Well, that's not going to help me. I need you in front of us, not behind us."

Billy shrugged and held both hands out, palms up. "Sorry. It's the best I can do."

"What if we get lost?" Carrie asked.

Billy laughed. "You won't get lost. That's what I'm there for."

"They mark out the course a day or two ahead," Rosie said. "All you have to do is watch for the markers."

Carrie didn't look convinced. "Maybe we can stick together."

"Don't worry. You'll be fine." Rosie was beginning to wonder if asking Carrie to enter the race with her had been a good idea. Her sister hadn't been conditioning Zach as much as she should. It seemed the only reason Carrie had agreed to be in it was because she thought Rosie wanted her to. "You know you could scratch your entry if you've changed your mind about competing."

"No." Carrie turned to get back on Zach. "I want to be in the race. I've just never done it before so it's a little scary."

"Neither have I, but it would be cool to win it the first time." *Especially* if it meant beating their new boarder. Rosie gathered her reins and started to get back on her pony.

With a clatter of hooves, Abigail and Raja appeared suddenly over the crest of the hill, spooking Scamper. He jumped sideways pulling Rosie with him. She held tightly to the reins and struggled to remain on her feet.

Abigail reined Raja in. The horse stood, head high and nostrils flaring. Sweat dripped down his sides to the center of his abdomen and from there dropped onto the dusty trail. Abigail had been riding him hard. Raja pranced in place, waiting for the command to take off again.

"Looks like Raja gave your boy a fright," Abigail laughed. "You better stay away from us at the competition so he doesn't get spooked. The little scaredy-cat."

Rosie patted Scamper's neck to calm him. She glared at Abigail. "Don't worry; that won't happen. We'll be so far in front of you, you'll never catch up." She turned her back on the girl and mounted Scamper.

"Ha! In your dreams." Abigail tossed her head and looked around at the others who were all staring at her. "Well, toodle—oo! No time for socializing. Raja is anxious to keep moving." She waved like a beauty queen in a parade, then gave an imperceptible signal to Raja, and the horse leaped into motion. Before Rosie could say anything else, they were halfway down the other side of the hill.

Everyone stared at each other for a moment. Finally Billy spoke. "I remember when I thought Katrina was bad, but this new girl takes the cake." He shook his head. "What a piece of work!"

"I wish I could be there to see you beat her," Jared added.

Carrie stared down the hill watching Abigail and Raja. "He really is a great horse though."

Rosie nodded. That was the part that had her worried.

"Swing your partners, do-si-do!"

Fiddle and guitar music filled the air. Rosie sat at one side of a picnic table with Carrie and watched her mom and dad whirl around expertly as the announcer called out square dance moves.

The farm looked so different tonight. The girls had spent most of the afternoon stringing white lights for the party. Jared and Billy had helped their dad set up sound equipment. A large white tent contained enough food to feed an army.

Grandma was trying to teach Billy how to square dance, but more often than not he ended up heading the opposite direction of the other dancers, with a bewildered expression on his face.

Rosie pointed and laughed. "Billy is so out of his element."

"I don't see you out there dancing," Carrie said.

"Uh, no. I'm sure I'd do even worse than he is." Rosie was glad Billy had returned to Sonrise Stable and not left for good that summer. He was like an older brother to her. Before Carrie was adopted and Billy came to work for them, life had been so different. She couldn't imagine being an only child again.

Now with the cousins living so close, they were all like one big family—and it was about to get bigger. She looked over at Carrie, and both girls giggled about the secret they shared.

The music died down, and Billy and Grandma walked over to the girls. "I'm getting too old for this." Grandma eased into a seat beside Rosie.

Billy grinned. "I'm sure it didn't help that I stepped on your feet a dozen times."

Rosie could sense how much Billy loved her grandmother. She had become like the mother he never had. Billy's mom had died when he was born so he never knew her. Rosie wondered if that was why he had a hard time turning to God. Was he angry at God for taking his mother? She would have to pray for him more.

Rosie punched Billy on the arm as he sat down beside her. "You look a lot better on a mule than on the dance floor."

Billy took a long drink of raspberry lemonade and set the glass back on the table. "Gee, thanks."

Eric stood up in front of the group and tapped his glass with a spoon. "I want to thank everyone for coming tonight to celebrate our fifteen years of marriage." He put his arm around Kristy and pulled her close. "My lovely bride doesn't look a minute older than the day we met."

Kristy laughed, and Rosie thought her mom had never looked so beautiful.

"I'd like to make an announcement," Eric continued.

Rosie smiled at Carrie. They knew exactly what their dad was about to say. The family had discussed this for the past few weeks, but no one else knew yet, not even Billy.

"We have enjoyed our girls so much," Eric caught Rosie's eye and smiled at her, "we want to add to our family. We've found a little boy we'd like to adopt."

Billy's eyes widened. "Is he talking about me?"

Rosie looked at him trying to determine whether he was serious or joking. "Um. I don't think so. You're not exactly little."

Grandma patted Billy on the shoulder. "You've already been adopted by all of us anyway."

A little brother. Rosie had been surprised when she and Carrie found out about it, but she couldn't wait for him to arrive. It would take some getting used to though. The youngest ones in the family right now were her cousins, Jessie and Jamie, and they were only a few years younger than her.

"How old is he? When is he coming?" Billy leaned forward in his chair and propped his elbows on the table. "And why didn't anyone tell me about this?"

"He's three months old." Rosie studied Billy. Was he jealous about the baby?

"There's lots of paperwork, and hearings and whatnot," Grandma added. "I imagine the whole process will take several months."

"We were going to tell you, but when we started planning the anniversary party, we decided to wait and surprise everyone," Rosie explained.

"What's his name?"

"Gabriel James," Carrie said.

"Billy the Kid and Jesse James. I like it," Billy laughed.

Rosie rolled her eyes. "I don't think Mom and Dad will be too excited about that nickname." She jumped up from the table and grabbed a small silver gift box. "Come on, Carrie. Let's give Mom and Dad their present."

The girls had debated endlessly about what to get their parents. Rosie had her mind made up—a leather holster for her dad's new gun and a study Bible for her mom. But Carrie had argued that those weren't good anniversary gifts. Normally Carrie went along with whatever Rosie decided, but this time she stood her ground. She insisted that they needed one gift that worked for both of them.

When they couldn't reach an agreement, they consulted with Grandma. She suggested a gift certificate for a stay at a nearby bed-and-breakfast. Rosie wasn't convinced that her parents would want to get away from Sonrise Stable, but she had reluctantly agreed. When Grandma had taken them to buy the certificate, the owner of the bed-and-breakfast found the girls so adorable that she gave them two days and nights for the price of one.

Rosie held the gift behind her back while she waited for her mom and dad to finish talking to someone. Finally her parents turned to them.

"Are you two ready to be big sisters?" Eric asked.

"I'm already a big sister." Rosie nodded toward Carrie. "I'm exactly fifty-nine days older than her."

"I can't wait," Carrie said. "I've never been a big sister before."

"Your baby brother will be fortunate to have sisters like you," Kristy said.

"I can't wait until he comes," Rosie said.

"He's in a wonderful foster home right now," Eric said. "We'll just have to be patient as things work through the system."

Rosie was good at a lot of things, but patience wasn't one of them. She liked things to happen instantly, whether it was baby brothers or trail ride competitions. "Oh!" She had almost forgotten about the gift. She brought her arm out from behind her back and held out the small box.

"Here's your present. It's from both of us." Rosie hoped her parents would like it. It had taken half the money they'd earned taking care of Katrina's horse. It would take longer for her to save up for Scamper's new saddle now,

36

but her parents were worth it—and she hoped to win the saddle at the trail ride competition anyway.

Kristy unwrapped the gift and pulled out the card and certificate. When she finished reading it, she smiled broadly and handed it to Eric. "Oh girls! What a thoughtful gift. Thank you so much."

"You're welcome." Rosie was surprised at how much her mom seemed to like the gift. She could hardly remember her parents being away for even one day. "Will you be okay without us?"

Eric smiled and gently tugged one of her braids. "I think we'll manage."

Chapter 5

Off to the Races

Carrie tossed her backpack into the truck. She couldn't believe the trail ride was tomorrow morning. She and Rosie had trained for it most of the summer, but especially the last four weeks.

After the anniversary party, Rosie had created a strict schedule that increased the miles they rode each day. If Grandma hadn't insisted that she give the horses a day of rest on Sundays, Rosie would have had them training seven days a week. Carrie didn't believe she and Zach had any real chance of winning the race, so she wasn't obsessed with it the way Rosie was. In fact, now that it was almost here, she felt a little nervous.

They would leave soon for the two-hour drive to Stony Creek State Park where the ride was held. The girls, their mom, Grandma, and Billy were riding together, pulling the horse trailer with Zach, Scamper and Sassy. Eric would drive down a little later with the camper. They would camp at the park that night so they could be up early the next morning to prepare for the ride. Abigail and her family had packed up Raja and left for the competition earlier that morning.

"Come on! You need to get Zach loaded. We're going to be late."

Carrie turned to see Rosie leading Scamper toward the trailer. In some ways Carrie would be glad when the ride was over. Maybe then her sister would return to normal. Rosie tended to be a little on the bossy side most of the time anyway, but the past few weeks she'd been almost unbearable.

Carrie closed the truck door. "Check-in isn't until five o'clock tonight. I don't think there's any danger of us being late."

Rosie tied Scamper to the ring on the side of the trailer. "I bet Abigail is already there, scouting out all the trails with Raja."

Carrie patted Scamper and looked the horse over. Rosie had done an excellent job conditioning him. She'd never seen him in such great shape before. Carrie felt a little guilty that she hadn't worked harder with Zach. "Do you really think you can beat her?"

Rosie unfastened the back door of the trailer and swung it open. "I don't *think* I can beat her. I *know* I can—I mean we can." She walked over to Scamper and wrapped her arms around his neck. "Can't we, buddy?"

Scamper turned his head toward her, wrapping her in a hug of his own. Carrie thought she could see a sparkle in his eye. She hoped Rosie and Scamper would win the race.

"Are you going to stand there gawking all day or are you going to go get your horse?"

Carrie stood up ramrod straight and saluted Rosie. "I'm going. I'm going." She trotted toward the barn and met Billy leading Sassy toward the trailer.

"Look out. She's on the warpath this morning."

"What do you mean this morning? She's been on the warpath all week."

Carrie laughed and continued to the barn.

40

When they finished loading the horses and equipment, everyone piled into the truck. Carrie made herself comfortable in the middle of the back seat with Rosie on her right and Billy on her left.

Grandma, in the front seat, fiddled with a paper map. She adjusted her glasses and turned the map this way and that.

"Mom, can you put that thing away?" Kristy stopped at the end of the drive, trying to look past the large map Grandma held. "I can't even see the road."

Grandma lowered the map, but continued studying it. "I've never been to Stony Creek before. I don't want us to get lost."

"Lost?" Rosie's eyes widened, and she leaned as far forward as her seat belt permitted. "We're not going to get lost are we? If we miss the check-in, we'll both be disqualified."

Kristy eased the truck and trailer onto the country road. "No. We're not going to get lost. I have the GPS set."

"Oh." Rosie leaned back in her seat. "Okay."

"Unless the GPS malfunctions," Billy said. "Or maybe it will be so remote in that area, we'll lose the signal."

Rosie jerked forward again. "What? Mom, could that really happen?"

Grandma turned and frowned. "That's not helpful, Billy."

He put his hands up. "Hey, I was just trying to be funny."

"We aren't going to lose the signal—and we're not going to get lost," Kristy reassured her.

"Besides, I have this." Grandma waved the map. "No signal required."

"Can I see that?" Rosie asked.

Grandma tried to refold the map, but couldn't get it just right. Finally she pressed it together the best she could and tossed it back to Rosie.

Carrie looked over at the map her sister was engrossed in, but she couldn't make heads or tails of it. She fished around in her backpack and pulled out a set of papers that were stapled together. "Um, do you guys want to hear—"

Grandma turned around in her seat. "I'm sorry, Carrie. What did you say?"

"Well—I was wondering if you wanted to hear my story—but if you don't, that's okay." She started to stuff the pages back into the pack.

Billy looked at her. "How long is that thing?"

Carrie swatted at him with the papers.

Grandma frowned at Billy again. "Of course we want to hear it, Carrie."

Kristy nodded. "Yes. We'd love to hear it. Go ahead."

Carrie smiled. "It's all about our animals." She propped the story up on her knees and began to read.

The Adventurous Convention

by Carrie Jackson

Scamper - Rosie's black & white pinto gelding

Zach - Carrie's palomino gelding

Patches - Jessie's pinto mare

Pearl - Jamie's pinto mare

Sassy - Billy's brown mule

Majestic - nurse mare colt

Charley - small chestnut pony

June Bug - bob-tailed calico cat

CHEO - Christian Home Educators of Ohio

"What in the world are you doing?" whinnied Zach as he watched the foal, Majestic, paw at a piece of white paper.

"Shhh, don't distract me, Zach, old boy. I'm filling out my registration for tomorrow's CHEO convention." Majestic continued to paw at the paper leaving dirty smudge marks all over it.

Zach rolled his eyes. "Oh brother, you've got to be kidding."

Charley moseyed over to investigate whatever his friend, Majestic, was working on so diligently. "What's a CHEO convention?" The pony tugged on one corner of the paper.

"Don't eat it, Charley!" squealed Majestic. "I'll never get to go if you ruin my registration form."

"Whatever." Charley shook his head and bit Majestic instead of the paper. Just then a loud, thundering noise and the pounding of the earth captured everyone's attention. The horses scattered every which way as Scamper galloped toward them.

"Alright, what's going on here?" the stocky black-and-white gelding snorted.

Majestic lowered his head to point to the crumpled paper at his feet. "I want to go to the CHEO convention."

"That's an interesting idea, little one," Scamper responded in a fatherly tone, "but you should have consulted with me first! Since you are so young and inexperienced I forbid you to—"

"Waaah!" Majestic burst into large foal-ish tears.

Scamper nudged the foal's shoulder with his head. "Tarnation, boy! You didn't let me finish. I was going to say that you can't go by yourself."

Majestic raised his head and looked at Scamper. "Really? You mean I can go?"

"No way," Zach protested, "I'm not going. I've heard the food there is terrible, and besides it all sounds too much like work. I'd probably go lame anyway. You know how my trick knee gives out on me all the time. I'm staying right here so I can just eat all day."

"Suit yourself." Scamper looked around at the other animals in the barnyard. "What about the rest of you?"

"I don't know what a CHEO convention is," Charley whined, pushing his way into the center of the herd.

"Well, I don't know exactly either," replied Majestic, "but my masters, Rosie and Carrie, think it's great. It's all about homeschooling, and you know they've been trying to homeschool me. Maybe I can learn something if I go."

"I'm already more advanced than you," boasted Charley, "but it sounds like a great adventure. I'll go."

Sassy, who believed herself to be Majestic's adopted mother, nibbled at the foal's withers. "I could never let my baby go that far without me. I'll go too."

Patches and Pearl, the twins' pinto mares stepped up beside Scamper.

"Enn he he he." Patches pawed and stomped her right foot. "Let us go too!"

"Yes, what about us?" pleaded Pearl. The mare looked hopefully at Scamper.

"No, we don't have room for you two," Scamper announced decisively. "You'll have to stay home."

"Waaah," cried Patches and Pearl together.

"Deal with it!" Scamper whirled around and cocked a hind leg as if to kick at them. The mares got the hint and scooted off to graze in the pasture. Zach followed after them.

Scamper motioned for the others to join him in the barn to plan the details of their trip.

Sassy rested her large head on one of the stall doors. "Are we going to walk there?"

"How ridiculous," snorted Scamper. "You've obviously never been to CHEO."

Sassy shook her head back and forth making her big ears flap like a helicopter. "Have you?"

Scamper reached over and bit the mule on the hindquarters for being so disrespectful. Sassy squealed and moved away from him.

"If we walk, we'll be so exhausted by the time we arrive we won't make it even halfway around the exhibit hall." Scamper spotted a bucket in the aisle and lowered his head to check for any leftover grain. Finding none, he returned his attention to the group. "No, the only way to go is by trailer."

"But who will drive us?" asked Sassy. She made sure she was out of Scamper's range in case he found her question stupid and tried to bite her again.

Suddenly there was a loud noise from the rafters directly above them. "Meeeooow. Meeeeooow." The horses raised their heads and saw June Bug, the cat, looking smugly down at them.

"I will. I will," she purred proudly. "I will drive you to CHEO."

Majestic pranced around the barn aisle. "Yahoo! We can go!"

"All right. It's settled," Scamper proclaimed. "Everyone get a good night's sleep. We'll leave at six o'clock tomorrow morning."

June Bug padded off to get the truck and trailer ready for their adventure.

* * *

Sassy was up with the sun the next morning, busily applying hair gel to her mane and tail.

Charley looked at the mule's left side, then walked over to her right. He shook his head. "Why are you putting that goopy stuff all over you?"

Sassy worked hard on a particularly tangled area of her tail. "It makes me look even more beautiful."

"Oh. I don't need any then. I'm quite handsome just the way I am." The pony arched his neck and pranced in circles around her.

"All equines into the trailer!" commanded June Bug in her bossiest voice. "Let's get this show on the—"

"W-a-i-t a minute!" Scamper glared at the cat. "I'm the one in charge here." He stared down each of the other animals to make sure none of them moved a hoof or paw until he said so. "Everyone into the trailer," he finally ordered. "Let's get this show on the road!"

"Oh brother," sighed June Bug. "This is going to be a long trip." The cat leaped into the driver's seat of the truck and maneuvered the trailer around the numerous potholes in the driveway. The cat, three horses, and Sassy were on their way to CHEO.

"Do you know where you're going?" Scamper whinnied out the trailer window to June Bug.

"Of course," June Bug growled back. "I've got my GPS right beside me. Now, no more backseat driving. Leave everything to me, and we'll be there in no time."

The horses admired the scenery as they traveled to downtown Columbus, Ohio. None of them seemed to notice the honking horns and shouts from irritated drivers as June Bug cruised along at 25 mph on Route 270. Finally

she exited the freeway and made a left turn
onto Broad Street.

Sassy peered through the open slats in the
side of the trailer. "This is sure a lot
different than where we live."

Majestic had to jump up a little to see
out. "What are all those things?" He nodded
to something beside the road.

Charley was so short he stood on his hind
legs with his front hooves up against the
side of the trailer in order to see out.
"Those are gas stations. I can't believe you
don't know what a gas station is!" He pointed
a hoof. "You see those hoses?"

Majestic nodded.

"They're full of grain," Charley replied
knowingly. "All you do is put the hose in
your mouth, push a button, and you can eat as

much as you want. When I was little, my mom told me all about them."

Majestic's mouth began to water. He reared up again and shouted, "Hey, June Bug, can we stop at the next gas station? I'm starving."

"Tough stuff," June Bug snapped back. "I'm not stopping anywhere. We're almost there."

Majestic gazed longingly at the gas stations as they drove by one after another, but he was excited to learn they were almost to CHEO.

Finally June Bug pulled into the convention center parking lot. Fortunately the parking lot attendant was on break. They slipped right past the booth unnoticed. June Bug drove the truck and horse trailer to the back and found a suitable parking place. The horses exited the trailer and stretched their legs after the long ride.

"Oh, no!" Scamper cried loudly.

Majestic jerked his head from one side to the other, fearing that they were about to be eaten by a mountain lion or something. "What's wrong, Scamp?"

"I think we have to have badges," Scamper moaned. "I remember hearing Rosie say that you can't get into CHEO without a badge."

"Who's worried about some silly old badges?" Sassy swished her tail. It had so much gel on it that it made a squishy sound when it hit her side, and it stuck there for a moment. "This is where my barging skills will come in handy. I'll lead the way and barge right through the crowds. Everyone follow closely behind me, and no one will notice that we don't have badges."

"It might work," acknowledged Scamper. "Hold on. I have money for everyone." Scamper grabbed the money he had stashed in the trailer and distributed some to each of them. "This is for books—not food!" He gave a stern warning look to Charley and Majestic. "Everyone meet back here at the trailer when you've finished shopping."

Sassy pranced along with an extra bounce in her step as if she were the grand marshal in the Thanksgiving Day parade. She led the group to the exhibit hall doors at the front of the building. People nearly knocked each other over in their efforts to get out of her way. One thing was certain—no one was concerned whether any of the horses had badges!

Majestic and Charley clip-clopped along right behind Sassy. They stopped when they entered the hall and gazed in amazement at all the educational booths and products.

Charley raised his head high and sniffed the air. "I smell popcorn." He looked around and motioned to his right. "I think it's coming from that direction."

"You better not," Majestic warned. "Remember what Scamper told us?"

"Aw, he's not my boss, and besides I'm practically starved after that long trip." Charley trotted off toward the snack area leaving Majestic behind.

"I guess I'll go to Good Steward Books," Majestic said to himself. "I've heard they have the best book selection and prices."

The colt turned to the left, quickly located the Good Steward booth, and began looking around. He spotted a book called Misty of Chincoteague that looked intriguing.

"That pony on the cover is adorable. I bet I could learn a lot from that book," Majestic said. "If only it wasn't at the very tip-top of that display." The colt pondered the situation for a few minutes. "Perhaps I can get the book down if I just paw a little."

Pawing at things was Majestic's solution for nearly every problem he encountered, however this time it was definitely not the right answer. When he started to paw, a mountain of books began to rain down all around him. The young woman working in the booth turned in the direction of the noise. When she saw Majestic with the books scattered all around him, she began to scream. Her piercing voice sent Majestic into a panic. He whirled around trying to escape, but only crashed into another book display. The frightened colt began to whinny frantically.

Sassy's ears pricked forward instantly as she heard Majestic's cries. She galloped toward him with Scamper close behind.

"I'll rescue Majestic. You locate Charley, and let's get out of here," Sassy ordered.

"Hey, I'm in charge. Remember?" Scamper complained. "You go get Majestic, and I'll find Charley. Meet us at the trailer."

"Isn't that what I just said?" Sassy snorted and shook her head. "Whatever."

Scamper suspected he might find Charley near the concession area and trotted off in that direction. Sure enough, as he turned the corner, he spotted Charley sitting, like a giant puppy dog in the middle of a mound of popcorn, munching contentedly.

"I thought I told you not to waste your money on food, young man," Scamper snapped.

"I didn't waste any money," Charley stood up and grabbed another bite. "A nice man gave it to me. He was making popcorn with that machine over there, and I ordered two big tubs. When he turned around to hand it to me, he jumped straight into the air." Charley looked up toward the ceiling and wrinkled his lip into a smile. "The tubs flew out of his hands and landed right here beside me. I don't know where the man went. I didn't even get a chance to thank him."

"You're impossible," Scamper muttered. "Come on, we have to leave. Majestic's in trouble."

"Leave already? I'm having a great time," Charley protested. "This place is so educational!" he added, hoping to impress Scamper and convince him to allow him to stay until all the popcorn was gone.

"Now!" insisted Scamper, and to emphasize the urgency of the situation, he bit Charley on the ear.

"Ow, why'd you do that?" Charley bent down to rub his throbbing ear on a front leg. The pain quickly vanished and since his head was close to the ground anyway, he scooped up another mouthful of popcorn.

Scamper moved around behind him and bumped the pony's hindquarters hard with his head. "Move it!"

Charley moved slowly, attempting to grab as much popcorn as he could on the way.

Meanwhile Sassy continued her search for Majestic. The colt's frantic whinnies guided her straight to the Good Steward Books. She spotted Majestic in the center of the booth surrounded by a pile of books and pieces of the broken displays. Several workers lunged repeatedly for the colt's halter, but he moved just out of their reach each time.

Sassy was certain they were trying to harm him. "Don't worry, my son. I'll save you!" She rushed toward Majestic, wheeling herself around so she could use her hind legs to kick books away and clear a path for his escape.

"Sassy! I'm so glad to see you," squealed Majestic. The sight of his adopted mother restored Majestic's confidence. He leaped over a pile of books and landed at the mule's side. "I was only trying to get that book *Misty of Chincoteague*."

"Oh, poor baby. Here's a copy." Sassy reached down and picked up a trampled book with her teeth. "Naw leth git ota hr," the mule mumbled, trying to talk and hang onto the book at the same time.

Sassy spotted Scamper and Charley running for the exit. She and Majestic galloped to catch up with them. They made their way out the front door and across the parking lot where June Bug was stretched out, sunbathing on top of the truck.

"Let's go, cat! Now!!" Scamper screamed at her.

June Bug jumped two feet straight up in the air. When her heart resumed beating, she dove through the window into the truck, started it, and began driving toward the parking lot exit.

Scamper, Charley, Sassy, and Majestic leaped into the trailer as it picked up speed. Once everyone was inside, Scamper pulled the door shut behind them. The truck and trailer headed back down Broad Street toward home.

"What's going on, guys? You interrupted a wonderful cat nap and scared me half to death. I think I lost another of my nine lives!"

"It's a long story," Scamper said in a tired voice. "We'll explain it all to you when we're home safe and sound."

"Safe and sound?" June Bug steadied the wheel with one paw and rubbed her forehead with the other. "Why do I feel like I'm going to get the blame for this?"

The End

Carrie set the pages down, almost afraid to look up. Would they think the story was stupid? Rosie had already read it, but she'd never shared it with anyone else. She caught her mom's eye in the rear-view mirror.

"Oh, Carrie, that is amazing! Your writing has really improved."

Grandma nodded. "You've captured the personalities of each of our animals."

Billy grinned. "I like how Sassy is the hero of the story. She needs a new name—like Sassy the Super Mule. She could have a superman 'S' on her saddle blanket."

Carrie beamed. Winning the trail ride couldn't feel any better than this. Maybe she could become a writer after all.

"Hey. Don't I get any credit?" Rosie said.

Carrie looked at her. "Oh, yeah, of course. Rosie's working on illustrations for the story."

Billy took the pages from Carrie and started thumbing through them. "You need more pictures of Sassy the Super Mule."

Carrie had tried to get Rosie to draw more illustrations for the story, but she had been too busy getting ready for the trail ride.

"And what do you call this?" Billy held up the illustration of the animals traveling to the convention. "Is that a horse trailer? It looks more like a camper."

Rosie reached over and yanked the pages out of Billy's hands. She pushed them forward toward her mother. "Here, Mom, see what you think of the sketches I've done so far."

Kristy shook her head. "Oh, hon, I can't look at them while I'm driving. I'm sure you did a great job though."

Grandma took the story and started looking through it. "Carrie, I love what you've done with June Bug. I can just picture her driving that truck. You've made the whole story seem so real."

Rosie slid back in the seat, crossed her arms, and looked out the window.

Carrie's smile faded. Was Rosie mad—or just back to thinking about the trail ride?

Chapter 6

Ready, Set...

"Are we almost there?" Rosie turned her gaze from the window to her mother.

"We're ten minutes closer than when you asked ten minutes ago." Kristy took one hand off the steering wheel, shifted in the driver's seat and stretched.

Rosie knew they must be getting close. It had been almost two hours since they left home. The truck groaned with the strain of pulling the trailer and three horses up another steep hill. Rosie couldn't understand why anyone would build a road with so many curves. Kristy shifted into a lower gear. She was driving so slowly Rosie was convinced she could get there faster riding Scamper.

"I hope the horses are in good enough shape for these hills," Billy said.

"Me too." Rosie nodded. They had ravines and hills at Sonrise Stable, but they weren't as steep or long as the ones they'd been driving through for the past fifteen minutes. Would Scamper be able to handle them? Rosie felt better knowing that Abigail hadn't been able to train in these conditions either.

She nudged Carrie who was dozing peacefully in the middle seat. "Wake up. We're almost there." How could her sister sleep at a time like this? Rosie had barely been able to sleep the night before just thinking about the race.

"There it is!" Rosie pointed to a small wooden sign by the right side of the road that read "Stony Creek State Park." An arrow pointed to their left. Kristy flipped on the turn signal, gradually slowed down and turned onto a gravel road lined with pine trees. Rosie wasn't sure if it was an actual road or a super-long driveway. It seemed like they drove for several more miles before coming to a clearing where rows of campers and horse trailers were parked. There was a large covered pavilion filled with picnic tables on the right at the front of the campground.

"Hold on," Grandma directed. "Let me find out where we're supposed to park." When the truck stopped, she stepped out and walked over to a table that was the hub of activity. In a few minutes she was back. "We have spots 99 and 100. They assigned the camping areas based on the rider numbers. We're in the back right corner."

Rosie scanned the rigs for Abigail and Raja. She spotted their huge camper near the front on the left side. Abigail must have been one of the first entries. That was fine with Rosie. Their campsites were as far apart as possible. Raja was tied to the trailer. Rosie figured Abigail had already ridden the trail. She couldn't wait to take Scamper out so she could see what the trail was like. It would be good for him to stretch his legs after the long trailer ride.

When they reached the back of the campground, her grandmother got out and guided Kristy as she backed the trailer into a grassy spot. Grandma signaled for her to stop. Kristy turned the truck off, and Rosie jumped out. A cluster of pine trees stood behind them. The driveway continued for a few hundred feet, then narrowed into a dirt path that meandered up the side of a forest-covered hill. In another week or two the leaves would start to turn, but for now everything was still green.

Billy opened the truck cap and lowered the tailgate. Rosie reached in and grabbed two lead ropes, tossing one to Carrie.

In front of the pines was a picket line. It consisted of a cable about seven feet above the ground stretched between two thick wood posts with rings every seven feet to tie the horses.

When their dad brought the camper later in the day, it would go on the other side of the tie line—a perfect setup. Rosie could look out the camper window and keep an eye on Scamper.

After they tied the horses, Rosie climbed into the back of the truck to drag out a bale of hay. Billy cut the twines with his pocket knife. Carrie held the mouth of the hay bag open while Rosie began stuffing hay into it. When it was full, Billy hung it up high where the horses and Sassy could all reach it. There was some squealing and stomping at first as the horses learned how to share. Scamper in particular didn't like eating with Sassy, but soon they were all munching contentedly on the hay.

"Grab your buckets," Grandma directed. "I'll show you where to get water for the horses." The girls located the buckets and followed Grandma down the road to a small shelter about halfway to the front of the campgrounds. Under the covered roof was a tall, narrow metal device. Rosie figured it must be a pump, but she'd never seen one like it before. She put her bucket under the spout and looked around for the knob to turn the water on.

Grandma smiled and pointed to a metal bar extending down one side. "This is like the pump we had on our farm when I was growing up. Move the handle up and down until water comes out."

Rosie grabbed the bar with both hands and pumped. Wow! This wasn't easy. The automatic waterers at Sonrise Stable had spoiled her. She was out of practice even carrying water buckets, let alone pumping the water herself. She was determined not to give up though and after several minutes, water began to gush into the bucket. Rosie kept the momentum going, stopping only when her bucket was nearly full. She moved it out of the way so Carrie could fill hers next.

"You're giving that water to your horse?"

Rosie turned to see who had spoken. She groaned inwardly when she saw Abigail. Another girl was with her whom Rosie didn't know.

"Why, hello, Abigail," Grandma said. "I see you made it safely down here."

Abigail smiled a sickeningly sweet smile. "Yes. Hello, Mrs. Watson. We've been here for hours. I've already ridden the entire trail."

Rosie stared into Scamper's bucket. "What's wrong with the water?"

"My dad says it's full of bacteria. I bet it will make your horses sick. We always bring our own water with us."

The girl beside her nodded. "We do too."

Rosie dropped down on one knee and looked at the water more closely as if she might be able to spot any bacteria floating around in it.

"Thanks for the tip, Abigail." Grandma waved to the girls as they walked away. "And good luck tomorrow."

Rosie dipped her hand into the bucket and held some of the crystal clear water in her palm. "Grandma, will this really make Scamper sick?"

Grandma shook her head. "No. Scamper will be fine. This water comes from a deep well. It's no more dangerous than the water he drinks every day at home."

Rosie looked up at her. "Why did you wish Abigail good luck? You always tell me you don't believe in luck."

"I don't." Grandma smiled and started out of the shelter. "Come on, girls. Let's get this bacteria-filled water back to the horses."

Rosie leaned over and picked up her bucket. Maybe her grandmother *did* understand how much she wanted to beat Abigail.

Carrying the heavy water bucket made it seem like it was twice as far back to their camping area. Every few steps water sloshed out of the bucket onto Rosie's pant leg. She was worried there wouldn't be anything left for Scamper to drink. When they made it back, she set the bucket down in front of him and waited. He lowered his head and sniffed, then returned to the hay bag.

Rosie put her hands on her hips. "What? You're not going to drink this after all the work I just went through?" She moved the bucket out of his reach so he wouldn't knock it over. She'd offer him a drink again later. "Can we ride now, Mom?"

"Not yet. You have to complete the check-in and the vet inspection. After that, you'll have time for a short ride before the rules meeting tonight."

Rosie nodded. She wanted to see what the trail was like and how it was marked.

"While you're over there don't forget to pick up your trail maps," Grandma reminded the girls.

Rosie grabbed the tack bucket out of the trailer. "Come on, Carrie. Let's get ready for the inspection."

The horses continued eating their hay while the girls brushed them. Rosie eyed her sister. "Are you nervous?"

"A little," Carrie admitted. "Are you?"

Rosie shook her head. "Not nervous, just excited. Now that we're here, I can't wait for the race to start."

Rosie and Carrie finished grooming Scamper and Zach and led them to the picnic area where the veterinarians were stationed. There were a few kids in line ahead of them so they let the horses graze while they waited.

When it was Rosie's turn, she led Scamper over to one of the vets. He asked only for her name, and her horse's name and age. He was one of the least talkative people Rosie had ever met.

The vet took Scamper's temperature, pulse, and respiration and wrote them on a piece of paper. He walked around the horse and rubbed his hand down each leg. Rosie walked Scamper in a straight line away from him, then turned and trotted back. The man wrote something else on the paper and handed it to her.

Rosie took it. "That's it? Scamper passed?"

The vet nodded and pointed to two women off to the right.

Rosie assumed that meant he wanted her to move on so she led Scamper away. One of the women walked up to her and took the veterinary paper, adding it to a stack on the table. She placed a smooth round rock on top to keep the papers from blowing away. The younger of the two women motioned to her with what looked like a giant magic marker. "Turn this way and hold him still."

She used the marker to paint a large red "99" on the top of Scamper's hindquarters. The number reminded Rosie that she and Carrie had just made it into the competition—the last two entries.

"Don't forget your trail map." The woman pointed to a box on the table.

Rosie grabbed a map and moved Scamper off to the side. She studied it while she waited for Carrie. The map showed at least a dozen lakes in the park. According to her grandmother, the whole area had been strip-mined for coal years ago and all the old mines had been turned into lakes.

After Zach got his number painted, the girls started back to the camping area. They quickly tacked up the horses. Rosie's Aunt Julie had loaned her a lightweight, Cordura saddle to use for the ride. It wasn't as nice as the endurance saddle Abigail had, but it was lighter than Rosie's Western saddle and would make it easier on Scamper.

"Do you have your watch?" Kristy asked.

Rosie nodded.

"Don't be gone more than forty-five minutes," Kristy said. "You need to be back in time for the meeting."

Rosie mounted Scamper and adjusted her reins. "We will."

Kristy raised an eyebrow. "You will be gone longer?"

Rosie laughed. "No, Mom. You know what I mean. I promise we'll be back in plenty of time for the meeting."

Carrie steered Zach over beside Scamper, and the horses walked side by side down the road that led out the back of the campground.

From studying the map earlier, Rosie knew the race started at the front of the campgrounds and followed this trail out the back, right past their campsite.

Scamper was excited to be on a new trail and wanted to go faster. Rosie had to keep reminding him to walk. She couldn't blame him; she wanted to go faster too. Maybe he sensed her excitement.

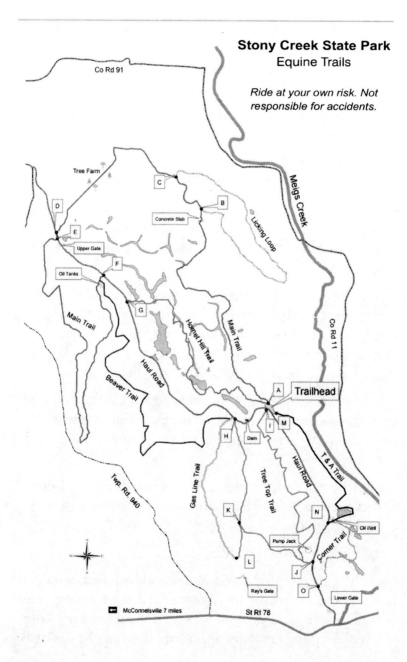

Stony Creek State Park
Equine Trails

Ride at your own risk. Not responsible for accidents.

Co Rd 91

Meigs Creek

Tree Farm

C

D

B

Concrete Slab

Licking Loop

E

Upper Gate

F

Oil Tanks

G

Main Trail

Hornet Hill Trail

Main Trail

Co Rd 11

Haul Road

Beaver Trail

A

Trailhead

H

Dam

I

M

Twp. Rd. 940

Gas Line Trail

Tree Top Trail

Haul Road

T & A Trail

K

N

Oil Well

Pump Jack

Corner Trail

L

J

Ray's Gate

O

Lower Gate

🚂 McConnelsville 7 miles

St Rt 78

"There's a marker." Rosie pointed to a simple white stake that had been pounded into the ground on the right side of the trail. A black cardboard arrow stapled to it pointed straight ahead.

"That's obvious. The trail doesn't go anywhere else," Carrie said.

Rosie laughed. "Yeah, it would be hard to make a wrong turn here—since there aren't any turns."

They rode together in silence until they came to a rock-covered hill. "It's a good thing we had shoes put on them. It's so rocky here they never would have made it over these trails barefoot."

Rosie loosened Scamper's rein and let him pick his own speed going up the steep hill. He scrambled up the slope half leaping, half cantering. Rosie stopped when they reached the top and waited for Carrie to catch up. A little further along, the trail split off in three directions.

The marker placed at the intersection clearly indicated they should turn to the right. Rosie reined in Scamper. "It's been about twenty minutes. We'd better turn around and start back."

Carrie nodded. "I'm glad we got to ride a little. I don't feel as nervous now. The trail is so well marked, I think even I can follow it."

"I told you you'd be fine."

The girls rode back to camp, unsaddled the horses and tied them to the picket line. Sassy squealed a greeting to her friends. Scamper responded with an impatient snort. Rosie offered her pony his water again, and this time he drained the entire bucket.

In the meantime, Eric had arrived with the camper. Billy was out collecting fallen branches for a campfire. When they finished taking care of the horses, the girls, their parents, and Grandma walked toward the picnic area for the rules meeting. The building was already packed with the kids who were participating in the race and their parents. They located an empty table at the far side of the pavilion and sat down.

Rosie eyed the prize table, which was covered with trophies and awards. Two endurance saddles sat on racks at either end of the table—one for the winner of the junior division and the other for the senior winner. It was the exact model she had been hoping to get for Scamper.

Rosie scanned the tables searching for Abigail. She spotted her several tables away. The girl was looking straight at her. She could see her mouth moving, but couldn't understand anything she was saying. Rosie shrugged her shoulders.

Abigail pointed to the prize saddle, then to herself, and mouthed one word slowly.

Rosie got it this time—"Mine." She frowned and looked away. She knew the Bible said to love our enemies, but she had never met anyone she disliked so much. Every encounter she had with Abigail made her all the more determined to beat her. The girl already had a nearly identical saddle. What would she do with another one?

One of the ride organizers stood up and began talking. Rosie focused her attention on him as he explained the rules and how the ride would be conducted. The meeting was short, and soon they were on their way back to the camper where Billy had a small fire going. They all grabbed chairs and sat around talking.

Rosie thought about everything she had to do in the morning. She planned to be up at five to feed the horses. While the horses were eating, the ride officials would visit each campsite to inspect the rider's tack and setup—how clean the area was, whether the horses had fresh water, and a salt block, even what kind of knot was used to tie the horse. Rosie didn't want to lose any points on the inspection.

At eight o'clock the senior riders would begin going out two at a time. Then at nine, the juniors would start. Rosie could hardly wait.

Chapter 7

Race Day

Carrie's eyes flickered open. She inhaled the familiar scent of freshly brewed coffee and pulled the blanket closer around her. It was too early to get up. For a moment it seemed as if she were in her room in the old farmhouse at Sonrise Stable.

When she remembered where she was, her eyes popped back open. It was race day! The bunk across from her was empty. Rosie was gone. Carrie jerked upright, stepped across the narrow aisle, and climbed onto her sister's bed. She pulled back the curtain from the small window. In the dim light she could just make out the shapes of the horses. They called back and forth to other horses at the camp—or maybe they were calling to their owners, demanding their breakfast.

Carrie hurried toward the front of the camper where the adults were seated around the small table drinking coffee and talking quietly. "Why didn't you wake me up?"

"We were just about to," Grandma said.

Kristy smiled at her. "Good morning, kiddo."

"Is Rosie already out there?"

"Yes." Eric nodded. "She wanted to wake you, but we wouldn't let her."

"She's obsessed about this race." Kristy shook her head. "There was absolutely no need for her to be up so early."

"Why don't you help Rosie feed and water the horses?" Eric suggested. "Then you girls come in and eat your own breakfast."

Carrie ran to get dressed. Minutes later she was back, pulling a sweatshirt down over her head. When she stepped out the camper door, it seemed like she had entered another world. The smell of smoke lingered from the previous evening's campfires. Fog hung in the air so thickly she couldn't see the truck and trailer that she knew were on the other side of the horses. It felt like a dream. The dampness in the air seeped into her bones, and she shivered even with her sweatshirt on.

"About time you got up."

Carrie jumped as Rosie emerged out of the fog.

"I thought you might sleep through the race. Come on. Help me get the hay." Rosie tossed her the hay net. "Billy's filling the water buckets for us."

As Carrie followed Rosie to the truck, a lump formed in the back of her throat. She swallowed hard, but it didn't go away. It just settled at the bottom of her stomach. She didn't see how she was going to be able to eat breakfast. Why couldn't she be as confident as Rosie? Yesterday after riding the trail, she had felt good about the race, but this morning the fear was back.

Rosie opened the door to the truck cap and climbed inside. She pushed several flakes of hay onto the tailgate and jumped down. The girls stuffed the bag full. Scamper nickered eagerly for his breakfast, and Sassy pawed the ground. Zach looked at his two neighbors as if reminding them to be patient.

Carrie pointed up to the tie line. "It's too high. We'll have to wait for Billy to hang it."

Rosie nodded. "Let's set out our tack for the inspection." She started toward the horse trailer, but quickly realized Carrie wasn't following. She stopped and looked back. "What's wrong?"

"I don't know." Carrie pulled a piece of hay out of the bag and twirled it between her fingers. "I'm not sure I can do it."

"Are you serious?" Rosie stared at her. "Of course you can. There's nothing to it. You just ride around the trail. We've been practicing for this for months."

Carrie stared at the ground. She didn't want to disappoint Rosie or her parents and grandmother.

"Do you want me to pray for you?"

Carrie nodded.

Rosie grabbed her sister's hands. "God, thank you for letting us be in this race. Help Carrie not to be nervous or scared."

Carrie felt Rosie give her hand a squeeze.

"Keep Scamper and Zach strong and healthy—" Rosie paused. "—and help me beat Abigail! Amen."

Carrie opened her eyes and took a deep breath. Maybe everything would be okay after all.

While the girls were setting out their equipment, Billy returned carrying two buckets of water. He set them down and grabbed the hay.

As he approached the horses, they pushed into him trying to yank a mouthful of hay from the bag. "Whoa! Hold your horses, you greedy little critters. Let me get this tied first." He made them each back up a step until he had the bag tied onto the line. Then he stood still and stared at the horses for a moment, making sure none of them moved an inch. Scamper tossed his head and licked his lips, but he dared not move. Finally Billy clucked to them. "Okay. Breakfast is served." He backed away, and they all tore into the hay.

Carrie wondered if she would ever be as good with horses as Billy and Rosie were. Maybe she shouldn't have entered the race.

Billy brushed off the hay clinging to his jeans. "Sassy the Super Mule needs to get energized for this race."

Rosie placed her saddle on a rack she had set up beside the truck. "Sassy's not even in the race!"

Billy frowned and raised a finger to his lips. "Shh! Don't let her hear you say that! She thinks she's in it just like Scamper and Zach."

Carrie laughed. "But you're just a lag rider."

Billy hurried over to cover the mule's big ears with his hands. "You two need to stop putting such negative thoughts into my mule's mind."

Rosie shook her head. "You really think she has one? Lag riders have to stay behind all the real competitors. How is the Super Mule going to feel about that?"

"The Bible does say that the last will be first," Carrie said.

"There you go." Billy uncovered Sassy's ears. "Did you hear that, girl? You're going to be first."

Carrie patted the mule's neck. "Maybe she'll do something heroic like in my story."

"Yeah." Billy smiled. "I can see it now. We'll both be famous."

"You're delusional," Rosie said. "All I know is that Scamper and I are not going to be last!"

Carrie set a water bucket in front of Zach and watched him drink. The sun had burned away all the fog, revealing a brilliant blue, cloudless sky. The inspection was finished. The woman had walked around their setup a few times, looked things over and jotted notes on her clipboard. Her face was expressionless so there was no way to know whether they had lost any points or not. Carrie still felt nervous, but she had managed to eat a little breakfast.

A horse and rider team trotted by, down the gravel road that led out the back of the campground. The senior riders had been departing in groups of two since 8 a.m. The starts were staggered every two minutes so riders would be evenly spaced over the trail. Each rider's start and finish times were recorded so their total ride time could be calculated later that day. The juniors and seniors started and ended at the same places, but somewhere in the middle of the course the seniors made a turn that took them on a route that was twice as long.

Carrie pulled the map out of her pocket and studied it.

Grandma walked up beside her, leaned over and examined the map. She placed a hand on Carrie's shoulder. "You have that thing memorized yet?"

"With all the turns and loops in the trails, it's very confusing."

Grandma nodded. "There are fifty miles of trails, but they'll have the course clearly marked. And you have Billy and the Super Mule following you." She nodded toward Sassy.

"I know. I guess I worry too much." Carrie folded the map and put it back into her pocket. She let out a shaky breath.

"You'll be fine." Grandma looked at her watch. "Only a half-hour before the juniors start going out. We better get Zach ready."

Everyone worked together grooming, saddling, and bridling the horses and Sassy. Whenever a new set of riders passed by, the horses whinnied eagerly as if they knew their turn was coming soon. Sassy added her unique voice to the greetings.

"It's nine o'clock," Eric announced. "The junior riders will start any minute now."

"We're at the end though, right?" Carrie asked.

Her father nodded. "Yes, you and Rosie will be the last two."

Rosie ran a comb through Scamper's mane. "I bet Abigail's in the first group."

That was a good thing, Carrie decided. It was best to keep Abigail and Rosie as far apart as possible. They had been so busy they hadn't seen the girl yet that morning.

Carrie checked Zach's girth, then slipped the bridle on over his halter. Normally she didn't ride with a halter, but it was required for the competition. A lead rope was attached to her saddle in case she needed to tie or lead her horse on the trail. She checked over everything one last time—a hoof pick and sponge were tied with rawhide laces to rings on the front of the saddle, and she had a water bottle and granola bar in a pack behind the cantle.

"Loose horse!" someone shouted.

Carrie whirled in the direction of the voice. A saddled, but riderless horse zipped past them down the gravel road.

People all over the campground were shouting out warnings or advice. "Look out! Loose horse! Someone catch that horse!"

Then Rosie pointed to a girl running on the road toward them. Abigail.

Carrie turned back to look at the runaway horse. Sure enough—it was Raja. He veered off the path and stopped to graze in an open meadow just beyond their campsite.

Billy held his hand, palm out, toward Abigail. "Stop! Don't chase him. You'll only make him run more. Let me try to catch him."

Abigail stopped in front of the truck. Carrie watched her take a deep breath and cross her arms. Rosie walked over and stood on the other side of Carrie, her eyes wide.

Billy tossed a scoop of grain into a bucket and walked quietly toward Raja. He stopped every few steps and shook the bucket so the grain made a rattling noise. Raja raised his head slightly and looked at him with one eye, then he resumed grabbing large mouthfuls of the tall, green grass. When Billy got within a few steps, the horse moved away, but he didn't run. Billy patiently pursued him and within ten minutes was able to catch him.

A crowd had gathered at Rosie and Carrie's campsite to watch. When Billy returned, he held out a single rein to

77

Abigail. "Looks like he stepped on his reins and snapped the other one." He pointed to a small section of a torn leather strap dangling from Raja's bit.

Abigail yanked the good rein out of Billy's hand, her face bright red with anger.

A race coordinator stepped forward from the group of people. "Alright, young lady, we'll give you time to repair or replace your tack, but you'll be moved to the end of the lineup."

Abigail nodded, and without a word, stomped off leading Raja.

"Okay. The excitement is over." The coordinator motioned for everyone to leave. "Let's have the next two contestants at the starting line."

When everyone was gone, Rosie turned toward Billy. "I thought Sassy was supposed to be the super hero. You should have used her to catch Raja."

Billy shrugged. "If I had ridden her, she might have scared him even more."

"Whose side are you on?" Rosie turned and walked back to the trailer.

Carrie watched her sister go. Was she mad at Billy for catching Raja? Now Abigail was going to be right behind them at the start of the race. Carrie felt that weird thing happening in her stomach again.

Chapter 8

Go!

Scamper snorted and danced in circles around Rosie. She held the reins tightly. That's all she needed was for him to get loose and run off like Raja had. There were only two more riders ahead of her at the starting line. Since Abigail had been bumped to the end, Rosie and Carrie were no longer paired together. Rosie would start the race with a boy she didn't know. That was bad enough, but poor Carrie was paired with Abigail now.

The girls had come up with a plan. Rosie would hold Scamper back until Carrie caught up with her so they could ride together. Abigail would probably blow past them early on. That was okay. Rosie didn't want Scamper to use all his energy at the beginning of the race. After the second checkpoint, she planned to turn him loose to go as fast as he wanted. She hoped that would be fast enough to not only catch, but pass Abigail.

Billy, on Sassy, was back behind everyone else at the starting line. He seemed almost as excited about his role as a lag rider as Rosie was about the race. Sassy was so sociable she would certainly want to join up with any horses in front of her. Billy would have to fight her the whole way around to keep her at the back.

Rosie adjusted her armband. The "99" on her arm matched the large number painted on Scamper's hindquarters. She looked back at Carrie. "You okay?"

Carrie nodded, but Rosie wasn't convinced. It was too bad she hadn't been assigned number 100 instead of Carrie. Her sister was already nervous enough without having to start the race with Abigail. She gave Carrie a thumbs-up, then heard her name called.

"You're up next!" Grandma motioned from the sidelines for her to move to the start.

This was the moment Rosie had been looking forward to for months. An orange traffic cone placed at the side of the gravel road marked the starting line. She led Scamper up beside it while a boy lined his horse up on her left. A volunteer walked briskly around Scamper, making one final inspection. The woman returned to her station beside the cone, looked at her watch, then called out, "Go!"

Rosie quickly mounted Scamper. She wasn't even fully seated when he took off at a trot. Normally she would have corrected him, but not today. Scamper was as anxious to get started as she was. His iron shoes made a crunching sound on the gravel as they trotted rapidly down the center of the road through the campground. Scamper didn't even look to the right when they passed their truck and camper.

Once outside the camping area, the trail sloped uphill and entered a forest. Rosie leaned forward and patted Scamper's neck. "This is the real thing, buddy. No more practice runs. I think you understand that, don't you?"

Scamper whinnied and pulled on the bit, wanting to go faster, but Rosie kept a firm hold on him. "Not yet. We have to wait for Carrie and Zach to catch up with us."

They climbed another hill, and Rosie glanced to her right. A stream ran through the valley below. The park was so beautiful. Rosie hoped her family could return and ride the trails some time at a more leisurely pace.

They hadn't gone far when Rosie heard a noise and turned in the saddle. Sure enough, there was the familiar dapple gray, bounding up the hill behind her.

"Look out! Coming through!" Abigail waved for Rosie to move aside.

Rosie glanced down at the narrow, tree-lined trail and yelled back. "Where am I supposed to go?"

She didn't move to the side—there was no room. There would be enough space at the top of the hill for Abigail to pass. But when she glanced back again, she was surprised to see that Abigail wasn't slowing down.

"What are you doing?" Rosie pressed with her right leg, trying to move Scamper as far to the left as possible. Raja was right behind them now. "You're crazy!"

The Arabian's left side scraped against Scamper's right. Rosie cried out in pain. It felt as if her right leg had been ripped out of its hip socket. Scamper flashed his head to the side, ears flattened and teeth bared. He nipped Raja's hindquarters as the horse flew past.

Tears burned Rosie's eyes. Her right hand flew instinctively to her side. She pressed down on her hip, causing the pain to ease a little. Up ahead, Abigail sat back down in her saddle. In preparation for the close shave, the girl had taken her left leg out of the stirrup, raising it over Raja's hindquarters like a trick rider. Rosie watched until the girl disappeared over the top of the hill.

Carrie came rushing up the trail and stopped Zach behind Scamper. "Oh my goodness! I saw that! Are you okay?"

Rosie groaned and motioned forward with her head. Her whole leg was throbbing. "Let's go up there where there's more room." They followed the narrow trail to the top of the hill, and Rosie gingerly dismounted. She tested her weight on that leg and took a few cautious steps. "Oh, wow, did that ever hurt! For a minute there it felt like my leg had been torn off of my body."

Scamper turned around and blew softly into her face. "I'm all right boy. Don't worry. We're still in this race."

Carrie shook her head. "I can't believe she did that. Are you sure you're okay?"

Rosie nodded and got back on Scamper. She settled gently into the saddle. The intense pain was gone, but her leg still felt a little sore. She signaled Scamper to walk. "Come on. We can't afford to lose any more time."

Both horses picked up a high-speed trot. Rosie began to post. Ow! Normally posting was effortless for her, but now it was a bit uncomfortable. She tried to sit Scamper's fast trot, but that hurt even more, so she kept posting.

They rode along a high ridge for half a mile, then came to a steep downhill. Rosie pulled Scamper down to a walk. He proceeded slowly and carefully down the hill. Grandma always said she thought he was part billy goat. He was so sure-footed, he almost never made a misstep. Rosie felt totally safe on him, no matter how steep the hills.

A handful of horses and riders at the bottom of the ravine were having problems getting their horses to cross a creek. Rosie watched them as she waited for Carrie to come down the hill. They trotted together toward the creek. Scamper and Zach plunged in without hesitation, splashing muddy water all around them.

Rosie laughed. "Maybe that will inspire the other horses to cross."

After they scrambled up the opposite bank, Rosie glanced back. One of the horses was tentatively putting one hoof into the water. "Why would you enter a trail ride if your horse was afraid of water? That creek isn't even deep."

"I don't know." Carrie shrugged. "Zach loves water."

"Remember when he laid down in Grandma's creek?"

Carrie laughed. "How could I forget that?" She patted Zach's neck. "I'm glad he doesn't do that anymore."

The trail meandered through the woods, then opened into a clearing. The horses picked up a canter and passed several other horse-and-rider teams.

"I wonder how far ahead Abigail is now?" Carrie said.

Rosie rubbed her sore leg. "I wonder how many more people she crashed into."

Carrie frowned. "You should report her."

"I'm sure she would say it was an accident."

"Yeah, but I saw it. So it would be two against one."

"It's okay. There's a lot of trail left. I can still beat her."

"Maybe Zach and I will beat both of you!" Carrie laughed and urged her horse to speed up.

Rosie smiled. If Abigail thought crashing into her would give her an edge in the race, her strategy had backfired. Carrie seemed to have forgotten her nervousness. Now they were both determined to beat the girl.

"Crossing ahead." Carrie pointed to the trail marker.

Rosie pointed to her right. "That way." The girls turned and rode back into the woods. The trail was so narrow in this section, they rode single file with Rosie in the lead. They couldn't go faster than a trot, and they slowed to a walk on the steep, rocky hills.

Rosie glanced back at Carrie. "I see why this is called Stony Creek. The stones aren't just in the creek; they're everywhere!"

After four miles, they reached the first checkpoint. The station was manned by half a dozen volunteers who jumped up from their lawn chairs when they saw the girls coming in. This checkpoint was a third of the way through the course. In another four miles there would be a second stop, then the last four miles to the finish line.

Rosie jumped down, forgetting about her sore leg. She felt a twinge of pain but quickly focused her attention on the task at hand. One of the race volunteers met her and began counting Scamper's respirations. Rosie watched Scamper's side and counted also. Another volunteer measured his pulse.

Pulse 90. Respirations 70.

Whew! Scamper wasn't even close to inverting. Rosie looked over at Carrie and saw her smiling. Zach must be okay too. Rosie's head felt like it was melting inside her helmet. She pulled it off and set it on the ground. She wiped the sweat off her forehead onto her sleeve, detached the sponge from her saddle and dipped it in a water bucket.

For a moment she considered squeezing the sponge over her own head, but the water in the bucket was milky white. It had obviously been mixed with a fair amount of horse sweat. She'd have to be a lot hotter before that water would look appealing!

Scamper wasn't particular, though. He sighed when she ran the sponge over his neck. She squeezed gently so the sweat washed down his neck and dripped onto the ground.

Next, Rosie grabbed the hoof pick. She examined each of Scamper's hooves to make sure there were no stones lodged in them. A stone bruise would definitely knock them out of the race.

The girls walked the horses for ten minutes. As soon as they were given the okay to continue, they mounted Scamper and Zach and set off on the trail again.

A quarter-mile outside the checkpoint the trail began to grow more difficult. Rosie was glad she hadn't pushed

Scamper too hard at first. He needed his energy here. The hills were some of the steepest Rosie had ever ridden. Up and down. Up and down. They passed through one steep ravine after another. She looked back to check on Carrie every few minutes and was surprised to see her sister sticking right with her.

Every time they approached a new group of horses and riders, Rosie hoped Abigail would be one of them, but so far they hadn't caught up with her.

By the time they reached the second checkpoint, the girls were nearly as sweaty as the horses. Rosie jumped off Scamper and grabbed her water bottle. She took a long drink, then pulled off her helmet and poured some of the remaining water on her head. A volunteer took Scamper's vitals, but Rosie didn't bother counting this time.

Pulse 100. Respirations 80.

Higher than last time, but not bad considering the difficult portion of trail they'd just covered. Rosie wondered how hard she should push him on the last stretch. He seemed eager to go, but she didn't want to do anything that would harm him.

Anxious to get back on the trail, Rosie looked around for Carrie. She saw two volunteers standing on either side of Zach. Rosie led Scamper over to them. "Are you ready?"

Carrie rubbed her eyes with her hand and shook her head.

"What's wrong?"

"He's inverted."

Rosie's heart sank. She stood, staring blankly at her sister. Carrie turned and led Zach away, and Rosie followed.

"I can't leave the checkpoint until he un-inverts or whatever it's called."

"Oh, rats." Rosie glanced at her watch. "How long will that take?"

"They said at least another ten minutes. Maybe longer."

Rosie knew she should offer to stay with Carrie, but a ten-minute delay would mean losing the race for sure.

Carrie seemed to have read her mind. "Don't you dare."

"What? I didn't even say anything."

"I don't want you to stay here." Carrie waved her away. "Go on by yourself."

"Really?" Rosie studied Carrie's face. Was she just saying that or was she okay with finishing the race by herself?

"Yes. Go. If Zach and I can't beat Abigail, then you need to."

"Are you sure?"

Carrie nodded. "Zach and I will be fine."

"Thanks, Carrie!" Rosie gave her a quick hug and leaped onto Scamper's back.

The ground flew by as Scamper cantered away from the checkpoint. Rosie felt bad that Carrie had to stay behind, but now she could concentrate on catching Abigail without worrying about whether her sister was keeping up. She leaned forward and patted Scamper's neck. "Easy, boy. Don't wear yourself out."

She spotted two horses ahead. Scamper seemed to notice them at the same time, and he kicked into a higher gear. "You really like this, don't you, Scamp? You feeling like Secretariat?"

They easily passed the riders. Scamper had so much energy that Rosie let him run for a while. Soon they would be back to the grueling hills where he would be forced to slow down. The breeze created from the higher speed hit the sweat dripping down from inside her helmet, cooling her a bit.

Scamper zipped past a few more riders. Rosie had lost track of how many they had passed now. Anyway, it was impossible to tell how they were doing in the race since the first riders had started an hour before her. She reined Scamper in a little and glanced at her watch. With the delay caused by Raja getting loose, it had been a little after ten when she started the race. She had set her watch to twelve o'clock then so she could tell her race time at a glance.

Two hours and thirty-five minutes, counting the checkpoints. That wasn't bad considering the difficulty of the course. Each rider's time would be recorded as they crossed the finish line. Any points lost during the event would result in time penalties. The final winners wouldn't be determined until later in the day. Rosie knew that, but she wanted the satisfaction of beating Abigail back to the campground.

Scamper trotted up a gently rolling hill. When they passed over the crest, Rosie spotted a single rider. Her heart pounded—Abigail. There was no mistaking that majestic dapple gray horse. Abigail didn't deserve a horse as nice as Raja. Scamper flattened his ears and sped up.

"You want to beat him as much as I want to beat Abigail, don't you, boy?"

Rosie gave the gelding his head. She leaned down low on his neck, and he surged forward. They were going to win the race. She was convinced of it now. The distance between them rapidly disappeared. Soon they were right behind Raja, coming up on his left side.

Abigail steered Raja to the left trying to crowd them off the side of the trail, but Rosie was ready for her. She guided Scamper to the right, staying far enough behind to avoid contact. Scamper tried to take the bit and run, but Rosie held him back. She patted his neck. "Trust me. It's okay. We'll outrun them at the end."

Rosie spotted a marker ahead. "Slow down a bit, boy. I need to see which way to go." But Scamper had no intention of slowing down. He wanted to run. Rosie looked down to get a better grip on her reins. It took all her strength to slow him even a little. When she looked up again, her jaw dropped. Abigail had swept into a right turn, leaned out of the saddle and pulled the trail marker out of the ground.

"Ha ha!" Abigail held the wooden marker out like a jousting pole. "No one is going to beat me!" She cantered a hundred feet down the right-hand trail and flung the stake to the ground.

Scamper made the turn almost as sharply. Rosie kept the girl in sight while she thought furiously. How could Abigail do that? Any riders behind them might make the wrong turn—including Carrie.

Should she stop and replace the marker? If she got off Scamper to put the stake back, there was no way she'd catch Abigail. There were only a few miles left in the race, and everyone had a map. The other riders should be able to find their way.

Rosie could feel her face growing hot. She loosened her hold on Scamper's reins and squeezed her legs against his sides. "Go get 'em, Scamp! We can't let Abigail win!"

Chapter 9

Checkpoint

"Oh, you have a palomino too." Carrie led Zach over beside a horse that had just entered the checkpoint. "He's beautiful."

"Thanks." replied his owner, a cheerful girl with blonde hair. "This is Nugget." She looked from her horse to Carrie's and back again. "They sure look a lot alike."

The two horses were remarkably similar in appearance. Carrie wondered if Zach thought he was looking in a mirror when he looked at the other horse. Now that she thought about it, Carrie realized she looked a lot like Nugget's owner. Their hair color was nearly identical, and they were both thin, blue-eyed, and about the same height.

"I was riding with my sister, but she already left. My horse inverted," Carrie pointed to Zach. "so I'm stuck in the checkpoint until he recovers."

"Aw, that's too bad." The girl loosened her horse's girth.

"It's okay. My sister is going to win the race."

"She is? Oh really? That's funny. Nugget and I think we're going to win it, don't we?" She patted his shoulder.

"It's a good thing my sister isn't around to hear you say that."

The girl sponged her horse down. "I'm Sarah, just so you'll know when they announce Nugget and me as the winners."

The girl laughed, and Carrie joined in. She liked Sarah already, and she barely even knew her. "I'm Carrie, and this is Zach."

Sarah pulled out a hoof pick to check Nugget's hooves. "Maybe we could ride together for a while."

"I'd like that." Carrie dipped a sponge in a nearby bucket and ran it over Zach's neck. More water seemed to run down her arm than onto the horse. "I better get back to walking him." She waved to Sarah. "See you later."

Carrie led Zach down a wide, grassy side trail. "Looks like we're not going to win this time, boy. I'm sorry. I guess I should have worked harder to get you in shape for the race.

Zach rubbed his head against her shoulder.

"You forgive me?" She patted his neck. "We'll have to let Rosie win this one."

Carrie reached into the pocket of her jeans and pulled out a mint. The cellophane crinkled as she unwrapped it. Zach perked his ears. Zach and Scamper were both crazy about mints. It seemed they could hear that noise and detect the peppermint scent a mile away. She held out her hand. Zach wiggled his upper lip back and forth and daintily took the mint from her palm.

"That's your secret energy pill to help you make it through the rest of the race."

The horse shook his head up and down and smacked his lips as he crunched the hard candy.

"See, you look more energetic already. Come on, let's keep walking."

Sarah rode up beside Carrie. "Do you still want to ride together?"

Carrie glanced at her watch and frowned. "I'd love to, but we still have about seven minutes until Zach can be rechecked."

"Oh. I can't wait that long if I'm going to beat your sister. I'll see you at the awards program tonight."

"Yes." Carrie smiled. "When my sister gets her saddle for first place."

"We'll see." Sarah waved and turned Nugget toward the trail.

Carrie continued walking Zach, giving him a sip of water every few minutes. She wondered how far back Billy and Sassy were. He had to stay behind everyone, but she wasn't sure there was anyone behind her now. Now that Rosie was gone, she would feel better if Billy was closer.

Finally it was time for another check. She led Zach to one of the volunteers and prepared herself for the worst. She was surprised when the woman said, "You're good to go!"

"Really?"

"Yep. You only have four miles to the finish. He should be fine."

Carrie turned her horse around. "Did you hear that, boy? We can get back on the trail." She looked around to see if there was anyone she could join up with, but there was no one else in the checkpoint.

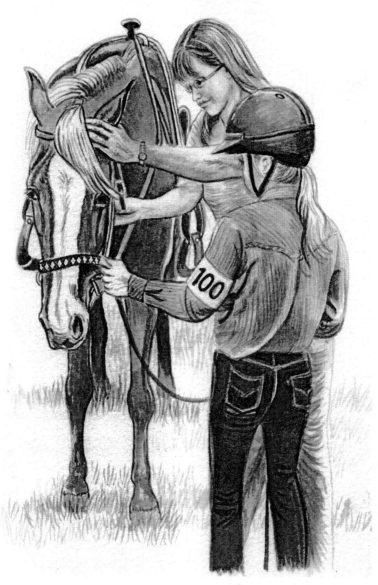

"I wish we could have ridden with Sarah." Carrie gathered her reins and mounted Zach. "Oh well, it's just you and me now. Maybe we'll meet up with someone on the trail."

She signaled Zach to walk, and they headed out of the checkpoint. Had Rosie caught up with Abigail? Her sister just had to beat the girl.

Now that Carrie knew there was no way to win the race, she was able to relax and enjoy the ride. She patted Zach's neck. "You doing okay?"

Not hearing any complaints, she interpreted that as a yes. They climbed a rolling hill. "This reminds me of the hills at home. You can handle this." Zach began to jog up the dusty trail.

When they passed over the top of the hill, Carrie saw an intersection ahead. She looked around for the marker. Zach continued jogging until they reached the point where the trails crisscrossed.

"Whoa." Carrie turned in the saddle, looking all around her. There was no sign of the marker, and no other riders were in sight. "What happened to the marker? Did we pass it already?"

Carrie caught her breath. "Stay calm. You can figure this out." She dismounted and reached into her pocket for the map. The empty mint wrapper crinkled, but she felt nothing else. Zach eyed her, eagerly anticipating another treat. She pushed him away and patted one pocket, then the other, then both back pockets. Nothing. The map was gone. Had she set it down somewhere and forgotten it? It could have fallen out when she gave Zach the mint. Carrie wracked her brain to figure out what had happened to it.

They were roughly a mile past the checkpoint. Should she backtrack and ask for help? She could wait here for another rider to show up, but what if there wasn't anyone left on the trail?

Carrie inspected the ground around the crossing. It was difficult to make out any prints at all in the fine dust, but the ones she could see seemed to be going in all directions.

Why had she told Rosie to go on without her? Carrie got on Zach and turned him back in the direction of the checkpoint. She stood still and waited several minutes. Maybe someone would come soon. Billy had to be back there somewhere, but she didn't want him to know that she was afraid. She closed her eyes and whispered a quick prayer. "God, help me find the way back."

Zach grew restless and kept trying to turn around. "What are you telling me, boy? Do you know the way to the campground?"

Carrie took one last look back the way they had come, then let Zach go. The horse turned around. He didn't glance to the right or left, but continued straight ahead on the trail.

"Are you sure this is the right way?"

Zach picked up a jog. He seemed confident he was heading back to camp. Carrie settled down into the saddle and tried not to worry. They couldn't be that far from camp. Rosie was probably already there. She couldn't wait to find out if she had beaten Abigail.

The trail led deeper into the forest. Carrie fought back the fear that tried to creep in. She glanced at her watch. It was a little after one. Her stomach had been telling her that. She reached into her saddle bag, pulled out the granola bar, unwrapped it, and took a bite. As she chewed, she tried to calculate how long it would take to get back to camp.

A loud squawking sound made Zach jump. Carrie grabbed for the saddle horn, and the granola bar fell to the ground.

What was that? She looked to her right and saw several large birds running for cover behind some brush. Wild turkeys. They didn't have those at Sonrise Stable, but she had seen them on other trails before.

Carrie slowly released the breath she had been holding. "Why are you so jumpy, Zach? It's just some old turkeys." She leaned over and looked down at the granola bar. Her stomach growled. "See what you did you scaredy-cat. I only got one bite of that thing. Oh, well." She signaled Zach to walk.

When they reached another junction in the trail, Zach didn't hesitate, but turned down the right branch. Carrie didn't even try to guide him. "I hope you know where you're going, because I have no idea where we are."

Shrubs grew in tightly on both sides of the trail until it became so narrow there was barely enough room for one horse to pass through. Zach had to step over small trees that were down across the trail. Carrie heard a rustling in the bushes, and Zach jumped again.

"Easy boy." She swallowed hard and stroked his neck, as much to reassure herself as him. "It must be those turkeys again."

Zach raised his head straight up. He sniffed the air and began to jig around on the trail. Carrie could feel his muscles tense like a coiled spring. She glanced slowly all around her, but she couldn't see anything unusual—not that she could see far, as thick as the brush was that surrounded them.

Up ahead, a small tree leaned diagonally across the trail. The top was lodged between the branches of a tree on the opposite side. Carrie had to duck low as Zach walked under it.

They continued on, although now Carrie was certain they were not on the right trail. She knew no one would plan the course on a trail this narrow. She considered turning around, but wasn't sure she could find her way back either. Maybe Zach was taking a shortcut to the campground. She decided to trust her horse's instincts.

The rustling sound occurred again, only louder this time. The bushes on the right side of the trail parted slightly. Zach snorted and reared, his front hooves pawing the air. Carrie screamed and leaned forward, frantically grabbing for the horn or her horse's mane—anything to keep from falling.

Zach whirled around and ran back in the direction they had come. Branches slapped against Carrie's legs as they raced wildly down the trail. She pulled hard on the reins, but her horse paid no attention.

The tree. Carrie saw it coming up fast. Zach scrambled under it, but she couldn't duck fast enough.

"Aagh!" She was falling, falling—then everything went black.

Chapter 10

The Finish

Scamper was more than happy to oblige Rosie's request for more speed. Soon he was nipping at Raja's heels like a pesky little puppy. Abigail turned in the saddle and glared at them.

At the next marker the trail wound back into the forest where they faced one of the longest, rockiest hills yet. Rosie watched Raja's hooves slip on the loose rocks. They were so close that, if he lost his footing, he would slide right into them.

She was relieved when they made it up that hill. They trotted along a narrow trail through the woods. The campground had to be just ahead. Rosie strained to see around Raja. She needed an opening wide enough to attempt to pass.

The trail opened out onto a road. That had to be the access road that came into the campground to the left of where they had started the race. This was her last chance. As the two riders burst out of the woods onto the road, Abigail stayed to the left. Rosie turned Scamper sharply to the right. The horses were so close Rosie could have reached out and touched the Arabian. Scamper must have remembered the bump Raja had given him earlier. He reached out and bit the horse on the neck.

Raja squealed and bucked. Abigail slid forward completely out of the saddle. When she slowed Raja to regain her seat, Rosie saw her chance. She and Scamper galloped down the road toward the finish. Rosie stared straight ahead not daring to look back to see where Abigail was.

She crossed the finish line and reined Scamper to a halt, her heart pounding with exhilaration. Rosie jumped down, beaming. She pounded Scamper's shoulder. "Way to go, buddy! I knew you could do it!"

She looked around. Where were her parents and grandmother? Rosie was surprised they weren't waiting for her at the finish line. "Just wait until they hear how well you did." She rubbed Scamper's sweaty forehead and felt his hot breath coming in rapid spurts against her arm.

All the participants were required to have their horses checked again at the end of the race. There was one horse ahead of her at the station so Rosie walked Scamper and waited for her turn.

A few moments later Abigail trotted into the campground. The girl dismounted and led her horse up alongside Rosie. Scamper flattened his ears and squealed at Raja. Rosie jiggled the lead rope to get Scamper's attention back on her. She glanced at Abigail and kept walking.

Abigail followed and leaned in closer to Rosie. "I should tell the race people how you moved that marker!"

Rosie stopped so suddenly that Scamper bumped into her. "What?" She glanced around to see whether anyone was close enough to overhear them. "You moved the marker—not me!"

"Hmph." Abigail took off her helmet and tossed her head. Her long, dark hair fell down around her shoulders. "Your word against mine. Who do you think they'll believe? The girl who won this race last year—or the newcomer?"

Rosie stared at her. Of all the things the girl had done to her, this was the worst. She couldn't believe Abigail could be that mean.

"And your horse is vicious." She pointed at Scamper. "He bit my horse twice." She pulled back Raja's mane to reveal a spot on his neck where all the hair was gone. "If they want evidence, there it is! If I tell, they'll ban him from ever competing here again. They probably won't let him be in 4-H at all."

Rosie felt sick to her stomach. Scamper wasn't vicious. He had never bitten a horse before. It was all Abigail's fault because she made Raja run into them at the beginning of the race.

"Keep quiet, and I won't report you." Abigail turned abruptly and walked away.

"Next." A volunteer waved for Rosie to bring Scamper over. One person checked his respirations and another his pulse. Abigail's words whirled around in her mind so violently that Rosie couldn't focus well enough to check Scamper's signs herself.

"Young lady, did you hear me?"

"What?" Rosie turned to the volunteer. "I'm sorry. What did you say?"

"Your horse is inverted. I've made a note of it here." She pointed to the paper on her clipboard.

"What?" Rosie shook her head. This couldn't be happening. Her world felt like it was crashing down all around her.

"Keep walking him to cool him down. Come back in fifteen minutes for a recheck." The woman moved on to check Raja next.

Rosie stood a few moments, watching Abigail to see whether she would tell her lies to the volunteer. When Abigail made a face at her, Rosie turned and walked slowly over to the cool-down area. Her parents and grandmother were waiting for her there, armed with buckets of water and old towels.

"Great job, Rosie!" Grandma patted her shoulder, then Scamper's. "I knew you two could do it!"

Eric loosened Scamper's girth slightly. He and Kristy dipped towels into the water and draped them over Scamper. "Walk him a couple laps, then we'll take the saddle off."

Kristy gave her daughter a hug. "We're all proud of you!" She stroked Scamper's forehead. "And you too, boy. I knew you would take good care of Rosie out there."

"How far back is Carrie?" Grandma asked.

Carrie. Oh no. She had forgotten all about her sister. *Did Carrie make the wrong turn at the missing marker?* Rosie could see contestants continuing to come in. Maybe the marker wasn't such a big deal. Each of the kids had a map and should be able to figure out which way to turn.

Rosie removed her helmet and tossed it on the ground. "Um." Part of her wanted to tell them everything, but Abigail had warned her to keep quiet. Could the girl really keep Scamper from competing again? Rosie fully expected her sister to come across the finish line at any moment.

"She got held back at the last checkpoint, but she should be in anytime now."

"This is so exciting," Grandma said. "Of course they still have to total all the points before they can determine the winners, but I think you have a good chance of winning the junior division."

Rosie managed a weak smile. For the first time since she had heard about the race months ago, she didn't care whether she won or not. She turned Scamper and walked around the roped-off area designated for cooling the horses down. As she walked, she considered what she should do. "It's not your fault." She patted Scamper. "You shouldn't be punished."

It would be ten more minutes before she could take Scamper for the next check. At the back, right corner, they turned and walked along the long side that faced the finish line. Rosie stared at the spot where the trail came out of the woods onto the road. *Come on, Carrie. Come on.*

It had probably just taken her longer than expected to get out of the checkpoint, Rosie reasoned. They walked another lap, then stopped by the bucket station again. Her dad removed the saddle, while her mom and grandmother pulled the towels off, soaked them, and placed them over Scamper's neck and back.

Rosie resumed walking until it was time to check Scamper. This time she counted the respirations with the volunteer. She checked his pulse from the inside of his knee, while the volunteer checked it under his jaw. Her numbers agreed with the volunteer's. Scamper was no longer inverted, but she still had to walk him another fifteen minutes, and then return for one last check. By then Carrie would certainly be back.

More cool, wet towels. More walking. Change towels. Walk again. The next fifteen minutes dragged by.

Every time she made the turn where the trail came into view, Rosie couldn't take her eyes off the spot where it opened onto the road. *Come on, Carrie. Where are you?*

When they completed the last pulse and respiration check, Rosie could tell her mom was worried. Most of the other riders were already in.

Her parents moved to the finish line to watch for Carrie, while Grandma walked with Rosie back to the campsite. She looked sideways at her granddaughter. "Are you okay? For someone who might win this race, you don't seem very excited."

Rosie shrugged and studied the toes of her dusty boots. "I'm okay. Just tired I guess."

"Here." Grandma reached for the lead rope. "Let me take Scamper."

Rosie handed it over and walked on in silence. When they reached the truck and trailer, Rosie couldn't stand it any longer. She felt as if she would explode if she didn't tell the truth. She slapped both hands on the top of her head and looked up at the sky. "Grandma. We have to go get Carrie!"

Her grandmother slid to a stop. "What do you mean? What happened?"

"Oh, Grandma, I made a big mistake," Rosie wailed.

"Oh dear!" Grandma's face turned pale. "Let me get him tied." She hurried into the campsite and tied Scamper to the picket line, while Rosie ran to grab a flake of hay for him.

When Rosie returned, Grandma turned her around so she was facing her. "Now, what in the world happened out there? Spill it all."

"Come on, I'll tell you on the way." She grabbed her grandmother's hand and tugged. "We have to go back out on the trail and find Carrie!"

By the time they reached her parents, Rosie had explained everything to her grandmother.

A girl on a black pony came down the trail and trotted over the finish line. Billy followed right behind her on Sassy. "That's everyone," he called out.

"What?" yelled Kristy. "Carrie's not back!"

"What do you mean?" Billy pulled Sassy to a halt. "I was at the back of the trail the whole way, and I didn't see her."

Rosie's heart leaped into her throat. She stared at Billy. What had happened to her sister?

Kristy bolted for the trail, but Eric grabbed her arm. "Hold on. You can't just run off down the trail."

"Who's going to stop me?"

"Now, wait a minute. Calm down, everyone." Grandma quickly filled them in on what had happened on the trail with Abigail.

"Why that little…" Eric shook his head. "We'll deal with her later. Right now we have to find Carrie."

"I'll go back out," Billy offered. "Sassy is still fresh, and I feel responsible. It was my job to make sure no one got lost."

Eric turned to Rosie. "What about Scamper? Is he okay to take out again?"

Rosie nodded. "He'll be okay."

"All right then. I'll ride out with Billy."

Rosie ran to her father's side. "Dad, you have to let me go with you. I know right where she made the wrong turn, and it's all my fault."

Eric looked at Kristy, and she nodded.

"Okay. You ride with Billy on Sassy, and I'll go get Scamper ready." Eric started to walk away but stopped when a police car appeared slowly driving down the gravel road.

An officer held a bullhorn out the driver's side window. "Emergency! Everyone clear the area immediately!" He continued down the center of the campground repeating the same message.

Every time Rosie heard the word, "Emergency," her heart thudded. What was going on? Was her sister the 'emergency'? The police car reached the end of the campground, turned around and started back.

A flash of motion to Rosie's right caught her attention. A horse was running down the trail toward them. Whew! There she was—finally! But as the horse drew closer, Rosie couldn't believe her eyes. There was no Carrie—only Zach.

Her sister's horse threw his head in the air, whinnied and looked around wildly. The gelding spotted Sassy and trotted over to them. Billy jumped off the mule and grabbed him. Zach still wore a halter, but his bridle was gone. He was saddled, but had no rider.

From what Rosie could tell, he didn't seem to be injured, but the whites of both his eyes were showing. He was obviously very frightened.. She stared at the empty saddle. *Oh, God, what happened to Carrie?*

The police car pulled up beside them and stopped. The officer put down the bullhorn and spoke in a normal voice. "You folks need to load up those animals and get out of here."

Eric ran over to the car. "What's going on, Officer?"

"There was a whole pack of wild animals let loose twenty-five miles from here." The officer shook his head. "Some crazy man let them all loose."

Rosie gulped.

"What do you mean—wild animals?" Eric asked.

"Tigers, bears, lions…"

Rosie's eyes were riveted on the officer. She didn't know why anyone would joke about something like that, but it didn't seem real.

"What?" Eric said. "Are you serious?"

The officer nodded slowly. "Absolutely. Now pack these horses up and get out of here."

"My daughter's out there!" Kristy yelled and started for the trail again. Eric ran after her and held her in his arms.

The man stepped out of his car and walked over to Eric. "What? Is she on horseback? Is anyone else out there?"

"All the other kids are in. We were waiting for my daughter." Eric pointed to Zach. "Her horse just came in without her."

The man pulled out a handkerchief and dabbed his forehead. "That's good. I mean—not that she's out there, but that her horse isn't. No one knows when these animals ate last…" He glanced at Kristy and Rosie and didn't finish his thought. "Of course, they probably won't come this direction. I mean, I don't know. Never had to deal with anything like this before."

"We're going after her." Eric started back toward the trailer.

"I can't let you do that." The officer stepped toward him, but Eric was already gone, sprinting toward the trailer and Scamper.

Rosie thought she was going to be sick. Tears streamed down her cheeks. Why had she been so obsessed with beating Abigail? If she had stayed back with Carrie, this never would have happened.

Campers, trucks, and trailers were already streaming out of the campground. Grandma took Zach from Billy. "We'll lock him in the trailer."

Billy got back on Sassy and reached down to pull Rosie up behind him.

"No. I'm sorry," the officer said. "That girl can't go out there."

Rosie fought back the panic that threatened to engulf her. "I have to, sir. I'm the only one that knows where my sister might be."

He sighed and shook his head. "I'll radio for help, but I don't know when, or if, anyone can get out here. Everyone in the county, maybe the state, is out looking for these animals."

Grandma took Kristy's hand, and they walked over to Sassy. "Let's pray."

Eric arrived on Scamper as Grandma finished her prayer. He bent down and kissed Kristy on the top of her head and squeezed her hand. "We'll find her. You two get Zach in the trailer, then stay in the camper until we return."

Kristy nodded, wiping tears from her eyes. She and Grandma hurried off, leading Carrie's pony.

"I'd feel better if you at least had a gun," the officer said.

"I do." Eric patted a holster on his right hip. "Hopefully I won't need it."

"Do what you have to do," the officer said. "I'd do the same if my daughter were out there." He got back into the car. "I have to warn people in the rest of the park. Be careful now. I'll try to get back to help you search, but I can't promise anything."

Eric nodded to Billy. "Let's go."

Rosie gripped the back of Sassy's saddle tightly as the mule started moving. They had to find Carrie—and quickly!

Chapter 11

Back on the Trail

Rosie wrapped her arms around Billy's waist as Sassy clambered up a steep hill. The mule was leading the way back down the trail.

"Abigail moved one of the markers?" Billy asked.

"She didn't move it. She picked it up and threw it down the trail."

"That's odd," Billy said. "I didn't notice any missing when I came through."

Eric followed closely behind them on Scamper. "Someone must have found it and put it back."

Rosie cringed. She knew that was exactly what she should have done. If she had replaced the marker right away, Carrie wouldn't have gotten lost. In fact, if she could go back and do it over again she never would have left Carrie at the checkpoint.

An awful thought occurred to her. "If the marker was replaced, then that might not be where Carrie got lost. She could be anywhere."

"We'll start there," her dad reassured her, "and we won't give up until we find her."

Her father's confidence encouraged Rosie. She knew he would stay out there until they found Carrie.

"Maybe that police officer will send some help," Billy said.

Eric shook his head. "It didn't sound like we could count on it. Carrie probably just wandered off the trail, and we'll find her soon."

"But why would Zach come in without her?" Rosie frowned.

"I don't know," Eric said. "Keep praying."

Rosie had begun praying the moment she saw Zach return without her sister. Something awful must have happened for him to leave Carrie. Had he abandoned her, or was he coming in to get help? Maybe if they had taken Zach on the search instead of Scamper, he might have led them right to Carrie.

They took turns calling out every few minutes: "Carrie! Carrie, where are you?"

Rosie scanned both sides of the trail looking for evidence that a horse had gone off the path. She couldn't make any sense of it. Carrie must have fallen off. But she was such a good rider, how could that have happened? Had she been laying out there hurt this whole time?

Sassy and Scamper traveled as fast as the trail permitted. Since Rosie was a passenger her mind wasn't focused on steering a horse. Terrible thoughts bombarded her. What about those wild animals? Why did someone turn them loose? Could they have traveled this far already? The officer said they were twenty-five miles away, but how long ago was that?

That was the exact distance the seniors had ridden that morning. Rosie knew it wouldn't take an animal long to travel that far. But she couldn't allow her mind to go there. There was no reason to think the animals would come this direction. *God, protect my sister. Help us find her soon. And, God, I'm sorry for being so obsessed with winning this race.*

112

"There's a crossing." Billy pointed down the trail.

"Yes. That's it." Rosie was puzzled. The marker was there now. Who replaced it? And why hadn't she?

Eric turned Scamper around to face the direction Carrie would have been going when she left the checkpoint. "You're certain this is the spot?"

Rosie looked around again, then nodded. "Yes, I'm sure this is it."

"All right. She should have made a right turn here, but if the marker was gone when she reached this point, she wouldn't have known that. Let's assume she didn't go to the right. That leaves straight ahead or to the left."

"What if Rosie and I go one direction, and you go the other?" Billy suggested.

"I can't let you do that, Billy. We only have one gun so we need to stay together." Eric patted the pistol strapped to the right side of his belt.

"This mule has two deadly weapons—her back hooves."

Rosie knew Billy wasn't trying to be funny.

Eric shook his head. "Maybe so, but I still think we have to stick together."

Rosie gulped. Knowing her dad was worried about the animals scared her even more. She cupped her hands around her mouth. "Carrie! Where are you?"

They all listened in silence, but there was no reply.

"You've ridden with Carrie more than anyone," her dad said. "Can you think of anything that might give us a clue as to which direction she would take?"

Rosie surveyed the area again. She'd already made too many wrong decisions that day; she didn't want to cause them to go the wrong way now. "Oh, Dad, I don't know."

"If the marker was down when she came by…" Billy began.

"She would have looked at her map," Rosie continued.

"Then she should have turned right," Billy said.

"But if she wasn't looking at the map the right way, she might have thought it was saying to go to the left when it really meant go to the right," Rosie said.

"That's possible," Eric said. "One thing's for sure we're not going to find her by sitting here talking about it. Let's take the left trail."

Billy tried to turn Sassy around, but she stubbornly refused to move. "Are you sure we shouldn't split up? Rosie could ride with you since you have the gun. I'll be okay by myself on Sassy."

"No, Billy. I appreciate the offer, but let's stick together." Eric turned Scamper to the left and started down the trail.

Billy shook his head. "Sassy really doesn't want to go that direction." He had to apply his spurs to get the mule to follow.

Rosie was relieved they had settled on a direction and were moving again. She hoped they were getting closer to Carrie. Another awful thought struck her. What if her sister was unconscious? They might ride right past her, and she would never hear them. Rosie prayed more fervently, then called out again, "Carrie! Carrie!"

As they rode deeper into the forest, the temperature grew cooler. An occasional drop fell from the leaf canopy overhead and splattered onto her helmet. How could it be raining? There hadn't been a cloud in the sky earlier. Thankfully the trees were thick in this area and protected them from most of the rain.

Rosie hadn't brought anything else to wear. She remembered how hot and sweaty she'd been just a short time ago. It was getting so dark in the woods that it seemed like night, but she knew it had to be early afternoon.

Her dad signaled them to stop, and Billy brought Sassy up behind Scamper.

"What's wrong, Da..."

Eric waved his hand and hushed her.

Rosie grew quiet. Had her dad heard Carrie? She could hear birds singing, leaves rustling, and the steady drip of rain. She strained to hear more. There, she heard it too! Branches snapped. Someone or something was crashing through the brush at the right of the trail, heading toward them.

Rosie watched her dad slowly pull his gun out of the holster and aim it in the direction of the movement. She tightened her grip on Billy. She wanted to close her eyes, but couldn't. A blur of something large and brown leapt out at them from the brush. Scamper and Sassy both jumped sideways, nearly unseating all three riders. As he scrambled to stay on Scamper, Eric lost his grip on the pistol, and it fell to the ground.

Rosie was the first to regain her balance. Nearly paralyzed with fear, she looked past Sassy's big ears to see Scamper standing face-to-face with a mammoth twelve-point buck.

The buck appeared to be more frightened than anyone—temporarily frozen in his tracks. Scamper gave a huge snort, and the deer regained his senses. He whirled around and ran fifty feet down the trail before crashing through the brush to the left.

Rosie, her dad, and Billy simultaneously released the breath they had been holding.

Eric turned around. "You two okay?"

"Yep." Billy looked back at Rosie.

She nodded and bit her lip to keep from crying.

Her dad got off Scamper to retrieve the gun. He picked it up and set the safety back on. Fortunately it hadn't fired when it hit the ground. He dusted it off and slid it back in the holster before turning to Rosie.

"I shouldn't have let you come out here. Now that we know the general area, we're going to take you back to camp, then Billy and I can continue the search."

"No, Dad. Please let me stay," she begged. "It will take too long to go all the way back to camp and come back here. Besides Scamper and Sassy would be too tired to do that."

As scared as she was, Rosie knew she would feel even worse if she had to go back and sit in the camper and wait. She wanted to be there when they found Carrie.

Billy shrugged his shoulders. "I'll do whatever you want, but I think Rosie's right. I don't know if these two have enough left in them to go back to camp and come all the way back out here again. These hills have been hard on them."

Rosie knew her dad was trying to protect her, but she hoped he would change his mind.

Eric shook his head. "All right, but if this goes on much longer, I'm taking you back. We'll just have to locate some fresh horses."

Her dad remounted Scamper and turned him around. "Let's backtrack. I have a bad feeling we're going the wrong way. Maybe we should have listened to Sassy."

Billy turned the mule around, and they headed back the way they had come. When they reached the junction in the trail, they turned left, which put them on the trail leading straight out from the checkpoint.

Sassy led the way. The mule had a definite spring to her step. Rosie felt hopeful. This had to be the right direction. She called out again, "Carrie! Carrie, where are you? Can you hear me?"

She listened for a response but heard nothing. She kept a sharp lookout on both sides of the trail. Before they had gone too far, the trail began to narrow like the previous one had. Rosie frowned.

If this wasn't the path Carrie had taken, she might be anywhere in the park. Rosie didn't allow herself to think about the escaped animals. "Carrie! Carrie!"

Something caught her eye at the side of the trail. "Wait! Stop! What is that?"

Before Billy could stop Sassy, Rosie slid off the back of the mule and ran to the right edge of the trail. She bent over and picked something up off the ground.

"Dad! It's Zach's bridle. We must be going the right way!" Rosie's heart pounded.

Eric and Billy jumped down and handed their reins to Rosie. They tromped all through the brush on both sides of the trail, but didn't find anything else.

Rosie kissed Sassy's nose. "Thank you, girl. You were right all along. We should have trusted you." Sassy tossed her head, and her ears flopped back and forth. Rosie stuffed what was left of Zach's bridle into Billy's saddlebag.

"Let's keep going," Eric said. "We have to be getting closer."

They remounted and continued along the trail. The further they went, the narrower the path became. They encountered several downed trees that the horses had to step over.

Eric shook his head. "I can't believe she would go this far. This trail is almost impassable."

They stopped and stared at the overgrown trail ahead. Rosie's confidence began to wane. She leaned over and looked at Billy. "What does Sassy think?"

Billy loosened his grip on Sassy's reins, and the mule immediately walked forward. "Sassy says keep going."

Eric shrugged and had Scamper fall in step behind the mule. They rode for another ten minutes.

"What's that?" Billy pointed to a yellow object in the middle of the trail.

Rosie leaped down and ran to it. "It's Carrie sponge! We have to be close now. I'm sure of it. She had this tied to Zach's saddle."

Billy and Eric dismounted and again handed their reins to Rosie. She didn't want to stand around being a human hitching post when her sister might be close by. She looked around for a place to tie Sassy and Scamper so she could help search.

There was nothing in the immediate area except saplings and brush, nothing strong enough to tie a horse or mule to. The last thing they needed right now was for one, or both, of the animals to head back to camp on its own, leaving them all stranded, but she wanted to join the search!

Rosie saw a tree up ahead, leaning diagonally across the trail with its top lodged firmly in the V of a tree on the opposite side. "Perfect!" She pulled Sassy and Scamper's lead ropes from their saddles, attached the snaps to their halters, and led them toward the tree.

Chapter 12

Good News

Eric looked up from his search. "Where are you going, Rosie?"

"Just going to tie them to that tree, Dad, so I can help search. I'll be right back."

Rosie had tied Scamper's lead rope to Sassy's saddle horn since the trail was too narrow for the two to walk side by side. She led the mule, and Scamper followed along behind. Whether he was too tired to care or he understood the urgency of the situation, for once Scamper didn't mind being behind Sassy.

As she approached the tree, Rosie examined it to find the best place to tie the mule. There was a knobby part of the trunk at the height of her shoulders. That would keep the rope from slipping down.

"Whoa," Rosie commanded. Sassy stopped obediently. She wrapped the rope a couple times around the trunk and tied a quick-release knot. "There. You two can rest for a while."

She ducked back under the tree, patted Sassy and Scamper and started back toward her dad and Billy.

"H-e-l-p."

Rosie came to a dead stop. A chill ran from the back of her neck all the way down her spine. What was that? She slowly turned around and looked to the left and right. Was it Carrie, or had she imagined it? She walked back, running her right hand along Scamper's side, then Sassy's. Taking a deep breath, she ducked under the tree trunk and moved cautiously to the other side.

"Help."

"Carrie?" She looked around. Her sister had to be close, but the brush was so thick, she couldn't see her. Rosie walked slowly, searching to the left and right, half afraid of what she might find.

Then she spotted a splash of blue on the ground just around a bend. Carrie was lying on her side at the edge of the trail, almost hidden in the thick brush, and facing away from her.

Rosie started to run toward her, then stopped and ran back, under the tree, past Sassy and Scamper, shrieking, "Dad! Dad! Come quick!"

Her dad's head jerked in her direction. She jumped up and down and waved frantically. "I found her! Come quick!"

Billy and her dad were at her side in what seemed like an instant.

"She's back there." Rosie gasped and pointed. She was breathing so rapidly, she felt faint. She took a deep breath, then led the way back under the tree. "Come on."

Eric hurried ahead and dropped to the ground beside his daughter. "Oh, dear Lord. Thank you. Thank you." Tears dripped down his cheeks.

Billy stood beside Rosie. No one seemed to know quite what to do.

"Carrie." Eric put his hand gently on her shoulder.

Carrie moaned and rolled toward him onto her back.

Her helmet was cracked in the middle. Rosie glanced up at the tree and began to put the pieces of the puzzle together. Carrie must have hit her head on the tree and fallen off, but how did she get this far off course? And why did Zach run away from her?

Rosie was half-afraid to look, but she walked closer. There was a dried trickle of blood down the right side of Carrie's face from a cut on her cheek. Her forehead was swollen and bruised. Rosie knelt down beside her father. "Is she okay?"

"I don't know. We shouldn't move her in case she has a neck injury."

Rosie whispered, "Carrie, are you okay? We're here now. We found you."

Carrie's eyes fluttered, blinked, and finally stayed open, but they had an odd, glazed look.

Eric held onto his daughter's hand. "Where does it hurt, honey?"

Although her eyes were open, Rosie felt as if Carrie was looking right through her—not really seeing her.

Carrie struggled to sit up.

"Take it easy," Eric said. "I don't think you should try to sit up yet."

Carrie sat up anyway.

Rosie wanted her sister to say something. "Oh, Carrie. I'm so sorry for leaving you. I'll never do that again."

Carrie raised her hand to her head and felt the riding helmet. She looked around at each of them. "Where am I?"

"You're at the trail ride. You were lost," Rosie said. "Remember when you got held back at the checkpoint?"

Carrie turned to her. "Who are you?"

A cold fear gripped Rosie as she stared at Carrie's unseeing eyes. "It's me—your sister."

Carrie stood up and began to walk away from them.

"Carrie," Eric jumped up. "Where are you going?"

"Home." She took another step, then fell to the ground.

Rosie burst into tears. She had fought hard to hold them back all afternoon, but now they wouldn't stop. Billy patted her awkwardly on the shoulder.

Through eyes blurred with tears, Rosie watched her dad pick Carrie up in his strong arms.

He walked back to them. "We have to get her to a hospital."

Eric lifted Carrie into the saddle on Sassy, with Billy behind her keeping her upright between his arms.

Eric handed Rosie his phone. "When we get close, keep trying to call your mom or Grandma and have them arrange for an emergency squad to be waiting for us when we get there."

Rosie nodded and stuffed the phone into her pocket. Right now they had to find their way back to the point on the trail where she had made the worst decision of her life.

Eric walked along beside Sassy, helping to hold Carrie in the saddle.

Rosie led the way back on Scamper. If Carrie didn't recover, she didn't know how she would ever be able to forgive herself.

Rosie finally got through to her mother, and by the time they made it back to the campground, a rescue squad was ready for them. The paramedics hurried Carrie into the vehicle, and Eric and Kristy jumped in the back with her. Rosie wished she could go with them. She watched her grandmother turn and start walking toward their campsite.

Rosie knew they had to take care of Scamper and Sassy, but she was too tired to move. She stared numbly at the squad as it made its way down the gravel road. She pulled her helmet off and tried to wipe the tears away on her sleeve, but her shirt was as damp as her face.

The showers had passed. Now a steamy vapor rose up from the warm surface of the road, giving the whole place a surreal look. The campground was deserted except for their vehicles way at the back.

Billy guided Sassy over beside her. "She's going to be okay."

Rosie wished she could believe that. Billy's kindness only made her sob even more.

Billy picked at a dried patch of mud on Sassy's neck. "The father found the sheep that was lost."

Rosie searched Billy's eyes. "You mean Carrie?"

Billy nodded. "Partly."

Rosie sniffed and did her best to stop crying. Billy looked different somehow or maybe she just couldn't see clearly through her puffy eyes. She hadn't cried this much since her pony, Jet, had died.

"I get it now."

"What?" Rosie's head seemed trapped in a fog. She couldn't understand what Billy was saying.

Billy removed his helmet and wrapped its strap around the saddle horn. He ran his hand back through his hair and took a deep breath.

"When I was watching your dad out there—how determined he was to find Carrie. I don't know—something clicked, and it all began to make sense. I knew he would never quit searching until he found her. Then I remembered the story we read from the Bible, and I realized it meant that God loves me as much as your dad loves you two."

Billy got it! Rosie was happy for him, really happy. She smiled, but couldn't think of anything to say. She slid down from Scamper. Her knees were so weak she crumpled to the ground.

Billy shouted for Grandma.

Rosie got back on her feet and tried to brush the mud from her jeans.

Grandma ran to her side. "Are you okay?"

Rosie shook her head. She wasn't okay. She had never felt worse in her life. She fell into her grandmother's open arms. It felt good to be held, to be safe and warm.

Grandma stroked her stringy, wet hair. "Carrie's going to be okay. Don't you worry."

Billy took Scamper's reins from Rosie. Sassy was on his right and Scamper on the left. He patted the mule. "You did good today, girl. Now, let's get you two into the trailer."

Sassy rubbed her big head against Billy's side, nearly knocking him into Scamper.

After Billy had the two safely in the trailer, he met Grandma at the truck. "Do you want me to stay here and keep an eye on the horses?"

Grandma shook her head. "They're not going anywhere. They'll be safe in the trailer." She motioned for him to get in. "Come on. You're going with us."

Rosie was already in the passenger seat, so Billy jumped in the back. Grandma tossed him the GPS. "Can you get us to the hospital?"

Billy pushed a few buttons and quickly located the address. When the GPS finished calculating the route, he set the device on the console between the front seats.

"How long will it take us to get there?" Rosie asked.

Billy looked at the screen. "About twenty minutes."

Rosie didn't think she could wait that long to find out how Carrie was. "Grandma, she didn't even know who I was."

Grandma kept her eyes focused on the winding road, but she patted Rosie's leg. "It sounds like she had a really bad bump to her head. Maybe she was just confused."

Rosie hoped so. She prayed silently for her sister. Was Billy praying for her too? She hadn't told Grandma Billy's news. Should she say something now? Or wait for Billy to tell her? She looked back at him. He smiled. He really did look different.

Chapter 13

The Super Mule

Grandma followed the street around to the back of the hospital and located a parking place. The three walked together to the entrance.

Rosie stared at the sign over the door—"Emergency." That's what the police officer had repeated at the campground. It was a scary word. Rosie wondered if they had captured all the wild animals.

The hospital looked as if someone kept adding on to it. The building sprawled out in all directions on a single floor. She followed her grandmother down a maze of corridors that reminded her of the winding road they had taken to the park.

Finally they reached an area with a large desk in the middle surrounded by small rooms, each with a white curtain in place of a door. One of the curtains parted, and her mother stepped out. Rosie ran to her and hugged her tightly. "How is she, Mom?"

"Much better. She wants to see you."

"She does?"

Kristy nodded.

Her heart pounding, Rosie cautiously stepped inside the small curtained room. Her dad sat at Carrie's right.

Her sister was propped up in the bed with a clear, narrow tube taped to the inside of her left arm. Rosie's eyes followed the tube to where it connected to a plastic bag hanging from a metal pole. She looked at the white sheets and beeping machines and could feel the tears starting again. She walked up to the left side of the bed.

Carrie smiled weakly at her.

"How do you feel?"

Her sister gingerly touched the top of her head. "I have a whopping headache."

"Do you know who I am?"

Carrie gave her a funny look. "What?"

"When we found you on the trail, you asked me who I was."

"I said that?"

Rosie nodded.

"Of course I know who you are."

Rosie held out her hand, and Carrie squeezed it. "Oh, Carrie, I'm so sorry. This is all my fault…"

Kristy stepped up behind her and placed her hands on Rosie's shoulders. "You can explain all that later. She needs to rest now."

Carrie closed her eyes for a few moments, then opened them again. "I got lost so I let Zach try to find his way back."

Rosie nodded.

"Here's the crazy part." Carrie gave a little laugh, then winced at the pain. "I know this is going to sound stupid, but the last thing I remember was thinking I saw a lion in the bushes."

Rosie felt the blood drain from her face. Her parents, Grandma, and Billy all looked at each other with the same horrified expression.

"Excuse me, but I need to take her down for a scan." A nurse bustled into the room and began preparing Carrie to be transported. "If the results come back okay, the doctor may release her tonight."

Everyone stepped into the hallway. Kristy grabbed Eric's hand. "Do you think it's possible..."

"I don't know." Eric shook his head. "She was very disoriented when we found her. Maybe she just imagined it."

Rosie wasn't so sure. She thought about the story of Daniel in the lion's den. God could have protected Carrie the same way. That would certainly explain what had frightened Zach so badly.

"Tell them your news." Rosie nudged Billy.

Everyone turned to look at Billy, even some of the employees at the ER desk. A red flush spread across his face and neck.

Rosie listened as he repeated what he had told her earlier. She wished Jared were with them so he could hear it.

Grandma and Kristy took turns hugging Billy. Grandma's eyes dripped tears. They all moved to the side when the nurse wheeled Carrie out. Rosie walked alongside her for a few steps and squeezed her shoulder. She stopped and watched them roll her sister down the long hallway.

"Rejoice with me for I have found my sheep that was lost." Eric gave Billy a quick one-armed hug. "Today we have a double celebration. You can't imagine how happy I am for you Billy. We've been praying for you for a long time."

"Thanks, Eric." Billy smiled and backed up a little.

Rosie knew he didn't like being the center of attention. She sat down in one of the chairs along the wall. "Billy, remember when Carrie read her story, and you said Sassy was the super mule?"

Billy nodded.

"She really was today," Rosie continued. "It was like she knew which direction we should go. If we had listened to her, we would have found Carrie sooner."

"Yeah." Billy smiled. "She really is a super mule."

The nurse returned with Carrie a half-hour later and got her situated in the room again. Now they just had to wait for the results of the scan. Carrie looked at Rosie. "Did you win the race?"

The race? Rosie had forgotten all about it. She knew she wouldn't win—and neither would Abigail, but she didn't care. Carrie was going to be all right, and that's all that mattered.

Lost Sheep

"What man of you, having a hundred sheep, if he loses one of them, does not leave the ninety-nine in the wilderness, and go after the one which is lost until he finds it? And when he has found it, he lays it on his shoulders, rejoicing. And when he comes home, he calls together his friends and neighbors, saying to them, 'Rejoice with me, for I have found my sheep which was lost!' I say to you that likewise there will be more joy in heaven over one sinner who repents than over ninety-nine just persons who need no repentance."

Luke 15:4-7

In the story it's easy to feel the urgent need to find Carrie. She's alone in the wilderness, possibly injured, with wild animals on the loose.

That's not a situation we're likely to face; however most of us do have family and friends who are lost in a more perilous way: they have never surrendered their lives to Christ for the salvation and eternal life that only He can provide. Carrie's danger was immediate and physical, but to be lost spiritually is far worse.

Luke chapter 15 continues with a parable about a son who rebels and runs far from his father. Billy, in the Sonrise Stable series, has been patterned after that rebellious son— going his own way and not giving God a second thought.

Everyone at Sonrise Stable witnessed to Billy and extended God's love to him. Rosie and Jared in particular made every effort to help Billy understand that he needed to turn his life over to Christ. They were patient and persistent despite seeing little or no results.

God calls us all to be witnesses—ambassadors for Him. We are called to faithfully and lovingly present the truth of the gospel; however we are not accountable for people's responses. Some plant the seeds, others water, but it is God who gives the increase. (1 Corinthians 3:6)

After his money ran out and his life turned sour, the prodigal son finally "came to himself" and returned to his father. God uses different people and experiences in each of our lives to bring us to the point where we also "come to ourselves." We begin to see things clearly—our own sinfulness and our need for the loving Father who is waiting for us to run to Him.

If you are one of those lost sheep, I encourage you to stop going your own way and to turn to your heavenly Father. If you are already part of God's flock, I pray that you will become part of the search party, helping others find their way to Him.

Discussion Questions

1. Have you ever lost something important, like Rosie did in the first chapter? How did it make you feel?

2. When she was younger, Rosie lied and blamed something she did wrong on her grandmother's cat. Later her conscience bothered her so much that she had to tell the truth. In Acts 24:16, Paul said that he always tried to keep his conscience clear before God and man. Can you find other verses in the Bible that talk about our conscience? How can you keep your conscience clear? What happens when you do not listen to the promptings of your conscience?

3. What do you think about Rosie's plans for spending her money? She wanted to buy something for her pony, Scamper, as well as a gift for her parent's anniversary. How can you as a young person begin to handle money in a way that is pleasing to God?

4. Abigail is rude, arrogant, and mean. What do you think about how Rosie responded to her? What could she have done differently so Abigail would not frustrate and annoy her? It's easy to come up with answers to theoretical questions, but much harder to put them into practice in our own lives. Do you have an "Abigail" you need to change your actions and attitude toward?

5. Rosie and Jared witnessed to Billy frequently, even coming up with creative ways, like the talking Sassy, to try

to reach him. Are there people you could share your faith with? (appropriate for your age/gender of course) Remember to pray for unsaved friends and relatives as well.

6. Rosie was envious of the attention Carrie received, when it seemed the family liked the story she wrote more than Rosie's drawings. Romans 12:15 says, "Rejoice with those who rejoice, and weep with those who weep." Which do you find easier to do? How can you be happy for someone else's good fortune when things aren't going well for you?

7. In our culture, competition is considered a good and healthy thing. Competition seems to be a part of almost everything we do. How do you think God views competition? Does the Bible have anything to say about it? What are some good aspects of competition? And some bad? How did Rosie's naturally competitive nature cause trouble for herself and others?

8. Rosie made a hasty decision that ended up hurting her sister. She knew what she should have done but deliberately chose to do the wrong thing instead. In the story, Carrie wasn't permanently injured; however in real life bad choices may have more drastic and long-term consequences. Although there is forgiveness, some actions we take cannot be undone. What are some things you can do to help you make wise choices?

9. Carrie was nervous and a little afraid about the trail ride. How can we tell when we should persevere through things that frighten us or when God is using fear to stop us from doing something bad or harmful? How can we overcome

our fears? Philippians 4:13 and 2 Timothy 1:7 are verses that encourage me when I face fearful situations. Memorize these if you don't already know them. Can you find any other verses that address the issue of fear?

10. It was Eric's selfless love for his daughters that showed Billy what God's love for us is like. He had read about it and heard about it, but seeing it lived out in front of him was what made Billy understand. As Christians, it's important to speak the truth of the gospel, but our actions need to match our words. Write or tell about a time when someone you know performed a Christlike action.

State Trail Ride

Each fall in Ohio a competitive trail ride is held, open to 4-H members throughout the state who have taken the Trail Riding 4-H project. There are two divisions: junior participants must be ten to thirteen years of age, while seniors are fourteen or over. The senior course is twice the distance of the junior.

Participants keep a conditioning record for thirty days prior to the race, documenting the training they have done with their horses and receive points for presenting this at the competition.

Points are also awarded for horsemanship, the horse's level of conditioning, tack presentation, and veterinary inspection. I've taken a few liberties in the book with the race aspect of the event. There are time frames set for the ride, including earliest and latest completion times. Finishing too early results in penalty points as well as taking too long to complete the course. For complete details about the event see: ohio4h.org

The Wild Animals

On October 18, 2011, fifty-six exotic animals including tigers, lions, bears, wolves, and mountain lions were turned loose at a Zanesville, Ohio farm by their owner, Terry Thompson. The farm was twenty-seven miles from the location of the State 4-H Competitive Trail Ride, held on September 21 of that year. The combining of the two events in the book is fictional.

In order to protect the lives of people in the area, when capture attempts proved futile, forty-nine of the animals were destroyed.

The Sonrise Stable Series

Available at sonrisestable.com & amazon.com

CPSIA information can be obtained
at www.ICGtesting.com
Printed in the USA
FFOW05n0216070815